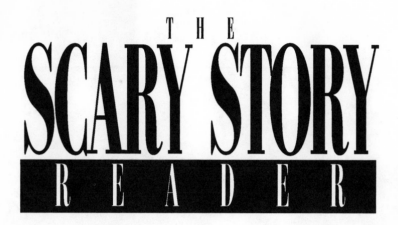

THE
SCARY STORY
READER

10/93

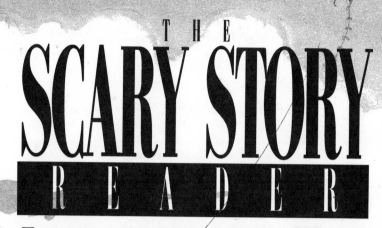

THE
SCARY STORY
READER

**FORTY-ONE OF THE SCARIEST STORIES FOR
SLEEPOVERS, CAMPFIRES, CAR & BUS TRIPS
—EVEN FOR FIRST DATES!**

COLLECTED BY
RICHARD AND JUDY DOCKREY YOUNG

INTRODUCTION BY
JAN HAROLD BRUNVAND

ILLUSTRATIONS BY
WENDELL E. HALL

August House Publishers, Inc.
LITTLE ROCK

LIBRARY OF CONGRESS CATALOGING-IN-PUBLICATION DATA

The Scary Story Reader / collected and retold by
Richard and Judy Dockrey Young
p.   cm.
Sequel to: Favorite Scary Stories of American Children /
edited by
Richard and Judy Dockrey Young. 1990.
Summary: a collection of scary urban legends and other
modern-day horror tales preserved by oral tradition, including
"Hook-Arm," "The Call from the Downstairs Phone,"
and "Give Me Back My Guts!"
ISBN 0-87483-271-3 (hb : alk. paper) : $19.00
1. Horror tales, American. 2. Tales—United States.
[1. Horror stories. 2. Folklore—United States.]
I. Young, Richard, 1946— . II. Young, Judy Dockrey, 1949— .
PZ8.1.S284   1993   93-24741
398.25—dc20   CIP

Executive editor: Liz Parkhurst
Project editor: Kathleen Harper
Design director: Ted Parkhurst
Cover design and illustrations: Wendell E. Hall
Typography: Heritage Publishing Co.

The authors wish to dedicate this collection
to the memory of Michael Olin Poe
and all the stories around the campfire.

This book is printed on archival-quality paper that meets the
guidelines for performance and durability of the Committee on
Production Guidelines for Book Longevity of the
Council on Library Resources.

AUGUST HOUSE, INC.   PUBLISHERS   LITTLE ROCK

Contents

Introduction

When the Lord destroyed the cities of Sodom and Gomorrah (see Genesis, Chapter 19), he allowed one family to escape, after warning them, "Look not behind thee." But Lot's wife did look back, "and she became a pillar of salt."

In a Greek myth, when Orpheus was allowed by Hades, king of the Underworld, to return with his dead wife Eurydice to the upper world, Orpheus was warned not to look back until they arrived. But he did look back, and his wife was lost to him forever.

In the modern urban legend "The Boyfriend's Death"—an alternate title for the first story in this book—a teenage girl rescued by the police after a night alone in a stalled car is warned, "Don't look back!" But she does look back, and she sees her boyfriend's mutilated body hanging from a tree above the car. In some versions, the girl's hair turns white from the shock.

There are three points to make about these stories. First, in general, modern oral narratives may recycle materials from older tales. Second, the "looking taboo" and its aftermath have a long history in folklore (including, also,

Pandora's problems after she looked into a forbidden box, and "Peeping Tom's" blindness after he sneaked a look at Lady Godiva).

The third point to note is that taboos in folklore are always broken, whether they occur in an ancient story or a modern one. The disobeying of the command creates the plot's tension, and as a result such stories, beyond being just scary, also describe the consequences of not following orders. Thus, contemporary urban legends—at least in part— continue the tradition of scary stories told in the past. This book contains a selection of such stories, ranging from ancient to modern tales.

What are urban legends? They are true stories that are too good to be true. Urban legends describe presumably real events, and they are usually told by credible persons— like your friends and family—who narrate the stories in a believable style. Although the characters in urban legends are ordinary people, the bizarre, comic, or horrifying incidents that supposedly happened to these people are extraordinary.

For example, in urban legends people do things like fill cars with cement, microwave their pets, get bitten by poisonous snakes concealed in imported garments, lose their grandmother's corpse from the car roof, mistake a rat for a stray Chihuahua dog, sit on an exploding toilet, steal a package containing only a dead cat, or drop to the floor of an elevator when another rider says "sit" to his dog, just to mention some typical stories.

Urban legends are too neatly plotted to be believed, even though they are told as true. A "legend," by definition, is any remarkable story that's unverified but repeated as the truth. An urban legend is one of these "true" remarkable stories with a contemporary (though not necessarily urban) setting and subject matter.

However, unlike accounts of real-life current events, nothing in these legends is extraneous; everything in them is relevant and focused on the conclusion. But urban legends are too odd and coincidental to be the literal truth, especially considering that the same stories are told in different times and places; yet, each telling of an urban legend is presumably about something that really happened to a "friend of a friend"—the presumed source, whom we folklorists refer to as a "FOAF."

Folklorist Linda Dégh explains that legends are believable because they combine a "verifiable fact commonly known to be true" with "an illusion, commonly believed to be true." That pattern fits most urban legends perfectly.

For example, the New York City sewers certainly do exist, and anything might be lurking down there; alligators are at least a possibility. The popular fantasy story claims that pet baby alligators were bought at amusement parks or brought home by New Yorkers from vacations in Florida and were later flushed down toilets into the sewers, where they have proliferated. This legend about alligators in the sewers combines truth and illusion in a memorable tale that's passed from person to person, and sometimes gets printed or broadcast, with continual variations.

Not all urban legends are scary; some are merely whimsical, bizarre or puzzling, and often funny. But horror stories are among the best-known urban legends, and these tales may be even scarier than older ghost stories because they are rich in the details of everyday life. They are also assumed by many tellers and listeners alike to have happened locally and recently.

As horrible as the details of a scary story may be, it's a real stretch to be asked to believe an older traditional horror story like "Spin! Spin! Reel Off, Skin!" or "Give Me Back My Guts!" These supernatural gory stories are told more for the pure thrill of terror than for any sense of verisimilitude. But urban legends are about topics like modern teenagers, cars, telephones, radios, and even digital watches (see the story "11:11"). Modern scary stories give you a jolt because they sound so much like actual accounts of everyday life, but with a twist!

Sometimes the twist involves comic relief; these have been dubbed "anti-legends." For example, read the stories "It Floats!" and "The Viper," which turn out not to be about violent crime—the "teaser" theme that's implied—but instead only about hand soap and window wipers.

These two anti-legends remind me of a recent story about a family that hears strange chirping noises coming from their basement; they fear that a flock of bats or of giant insects may have moved in on them. So the homeowners lock the basement door, seal up the edges with tape, and call an exterminator. The workman, however, checks the basement and quickly solves the mystery. Their smoke alarm battery had worn down, and the alarm had automatically switched into its "chirping" mode in order to alert them.

The modern legend counterpart to the older horror stories about stolen body parts is one I've named "The Kidney Heist." (See The Baby Train, New York: W.W. Norton & Co., 1993.) It's about a businessman visiting New York City who is mugged for one of his kidneys. Supposedly, an unscrupulous doctor needing the organ for a transplant operation surgically removed the kidney after luring the man to a hotel room.

The urban legend version of a story like "The Bloody Benders"—a tale of cannibalism—tells of some people who receive a jar in the mail full of a dark powdered substance sent by relatives who live abroad. Believing it to be a condiment or some other food product, the recipients of the jar try sprinkling the powder on casseroles, adding it to cake batter, or brewing it up as a soup or tea. None of these concoctions tastes very good, and only when the powder is used up do the people read the note enclosed with the jar and learn that they have consumed their grandmother's ashes which had been sent home for burial.

According to other urban horror legends, assailants hide under women's cars in shopping malls and slash at the drivers' ankles when they return. In a recent variation, gang members are said to accost women in malls and slash their cheeks as part of an initiation ritual. An older mall horror legend tells of a small child who is either abducted from or mutilated in a restroom.

Even if a mall shopper does manage to get home safely with, say, a large potted cactus purchased there, the plant quivers and buzzes (according to yet another popular legend) when it is watered, and it turns out to be infested with scorpions or tarantulas.

I hope that by calling all of these mentioned stories "legends" it is clear that, even though they are told as true incidents, not a single one has actually happened. But try telling that to someone who heard from a co-worker or family member about a friend of a friend (FOAF) who supposedly lost a kidney, fought off the ankle slashers, nearly had a child abducted, or barely escaped the flying spiders when the cactus exploded.

Or—in yet another wild tale—your friend has a friend who saw the ghost of a murder victim flickering across the screen on the videotape of a popular recent movie. But this story too has its counterpart, in older legends about spiritual images showing up in photographs.

Much of the appeal of these modern versions of old horrors lies in the matter-of-fact and cooperative way in which they are told. People do not repeat an urban legend word-for-word from memory; instead, they reconstruct the story from half-remembered details, unwittingly varying it slightly with each telling.

Often those listening to an urban legend have already heard something about the same supposed incidents, perhaps from a co-worker, or a store clerk or other stranger, or even on a radio or television talk show. Listeners then become tellers as they furnish new details or speculate about the truth of the story under discussion.

With contributions from everyone passing the story along, a legend grows. For an example of how the different versions of a single plot can result from this process of "communal re-creation" (a term borrowed from ballad studies), see the three variations of the vanishing hitchhiker theme included in this book.

First, the story "Last Kiss" is a classic version of the legend in which a ghostly rider simply returns to her grave, leaving behind a borrowed jacket. (The kiss from the ghost in this version is an unusual detail.) Second, in "The Lady from the Lake" the ghostly rider had been a drowning victim, and her identity is discovered by accident when the driver reads a newspaper account of her death. (Other tellings of this version mention that she left wet footprints in the car.)

The third variation in this book on the hitchhiker theme is "The Lady in White on Mount Hood." Here we find the motif of a warning to the driver. In some earlier versions the rider predicted something about a war or other disaster, but here she warns of the eruption of Mount St. Helens. (Of course, nobody heard the story before the eruption; it was told only after the disaster.)

All three hitchhiker stories have the same essential elements: rider, conversation, disappearance, and an identification or explanation. But each story-type developed in different ways. Eventually such stories acquire lives of their own, and then they can take root and flourish anywhere.

The drowned-lady version, for example, is found near Dallas, Texas, as "The Lady of White Rock Lake," but a very similar story is also the most popular hitchhiker legend told in Japan, where the girl is said to be riding in a taxi from the lake where she died to a nearby hospital. This Japanese ghost leaves wet footprints in the car, and is identified later through hospital records.

These scary stories, whether urban legends or traditional horror tales, will remind you of other stories you have read or heard, and you should feel free to tell and retell them in your own words. Let me encourage you to do so by giving brief versions of two of my own favorite modern scary stories that I heard recently.

First, from a reader in San Antonio, Texas, I heard one about a priest who, during his weekly visit to hospitalized parishioners, stopped to visit a man in the intensive care unit who was connected to several tubes and wires. Despite his condition, the man greeted the priest cheerfully. But as the priest stood at his bedside, the man grew visibly worse and seemed to be fighting to breathe. Gasping, he gestured for a pencil and paper from the table next to his bed, and he scribbled something and pressed the note into the priest's hand.

The priest stuffed the note into his pocket and rang for help, but the man died before anyone arrived in time to render aid. That night, as the deeply shaken priest prayed for the man, he remembered the note and pulled it out of his pocket. He unfolded it and read this: "Please, father! You're standing on my air hose!"

My second story came from a sheetrock installer who heard it on the job from another sheetrocker who started out by asking, "Did you hear about the local highschool football player who fractured his leg so severely in a game that when they took him to the hospital they had to amputate? But the doctor accidentally amputated the good leg! There he was with one broken leg and the other leg amputated."

The other workers stared in disbelief, until somebody chimed in with, "They must have sued the heck outta that hospital!"

"Nope," said the storyteller. "They couldn't sue."

"What! Why not?" the workers all asked.

"Because he didn't have a leg to stand on."

(Okay, so I fooled you with an anti-legend. Well, that's folklore!)

Jan Harold Brunvand
University of Utah
Salt Lake City
February 15, 1993

THE CLASSIC
URBAN LEGENDS

Urban legends are those remarkable, unverified stories repeated as if they were the truth, with contemporary settings and subject matter. City kids tell *city* urban legends, and country kids tell *country* urban legends. These are the most popular of the scary legends, told and asked for more often than any others we've heard.

Don't Look Back!

Folklorists call this story "The Boyfriend's Death." In some states it's known by the title "Drip, Drip, Drip."

TWO TEENAGERS DROVE out along a dirt road beyond the city limits to park. They stopped under a huge oak tree so the car would be hidden in shadow. That way, none of their friends could drive up and spotlight them to embarrass them.

It was a cold night, close to Hallowe'en, so they left the engine running and the heat on, with one window down a little for fresh air. The radio was on so they could hear the out-of-town football game. Just as the boy was about to make a move, the hourly news came on.

"Texas Rangers report that the sinister survivalist arrested for tax evasion yesterday has killed his captors and escaped. Although his legal name has never been determined from among his many false ID cards..."

The boy reached over to switch to a music station until the news went off. The girl stopped him.

The newscaster continued: " ... dressed in camos and armed with a huge hunting knife that he was carrying when he was arrested."

More news and a commercial followed, but there was nothing else about the Camo Killer. The girl was afraid, and insisted that they drive to someplace lighter to park. The boy put the car in gear, but it died—they had parked there long enough to run out of gas!

The boy's family were friends with the farm family that lived just up the road. The boy got out and took a metal gas can from the trunk.

"You keep the keys," he said, "and keep the windows up and the doors locked. I'll go across the field to that barn and borrow a gallon of gas. I won't even have to wake the family; I'll just tip their little tractor back and siphon some out of that tank." The boy shut the door and set off into the darkness. The girl locked all the doors.

The car got colder and colder, and as the wind began to blow, branches from the oak tree began to scrape on the car. It sounded like someone trying to get in! The girl slid to the floor and hid as best she could. She waited and waited and waited.

Sometime in the deep of night she fell asleep.

She awoke in darkness, and didn't want to turn on the key to see the clock. She was too scared to get up from the floor. The wind was still blowing and branches were still scraping on the car. Big, wet drops began to hit the roof of the car. It didn't sound quite like rain; it must have sprinkled while she was asleep, and now the drops were sifting through the oak leaves and hitting the car.

Drip ... drip ... drip.

Time passed, and she fell asleep once more.

Hours later, she awoke again. She felt awake, like it was morning, but she couldn't see out. It was still black as midnight. The sound continued. *Drip ... drip ... drip.*

She finally sat up.

It wasn't night, after all. The windows were covered with mud or something. It was a dirt road, but somehow it didn't seem possible for the whole car to be covered with mud. She found the keys and put them in the ignition. Sitting up, she turned the key and flipped on the windshield wipers. The wipers flopped back and forth, and cleared the windshield enough so that she could finally see out through the thick, red stain.

It was dawn and there was just enough light for her to see a car coming toward her with its lights off. It was a state police car with two officers in it. One was talking excitedly on the radio. They stopped, put on their "Smokey the Bear" hats, and got out slowly, drawing their guns. They approached the car.

The girl knew she was in trouble with her parents, but why would the police be drawing their guns? One officer came to her side of the car, looked in through the windshield, and put his pistol away. The girl opened the door and started to get out.

"Don't look back!" said the officer, taking her shoulders in his hands and helping her out. As she emerged, red liquid dripped off the roof onto her arm. She was looking at the stain as they walked to the police car. The officer took off his hat and held it near her face.

"Don't look back!" he said again. The stain wasn't mud ... it ... looked like blood. Blood. Enough blood to cover the entire car.

The second officer jumped behind the wheel of the

patrol car and revved the engine. The officer helping the girl let her into the back seat of the patrol car. He slammed the door and the driver sped away, leaving the first policeman at the scene.

"Don't look back!" said the officer in the driver's seat.

But the girl couldn't help herself.

As they roared past the car covered with blood, she looked up.

Dangling from the tree by his heels was her boyfriend. His head was hanging just above the car and his arms hung down, dragging on the roof. Blood ran down his face, down his arms, down the car.

His throat was cut.

Hook-Arm

To heighten the shock effect at the end, this story is often called "A Date Interrupted."

A YOUNG COUPLE out on a date parked along a dark country road to be alone. They were listening to the car radio and kissing and hugging. Suddenly the music was interrupted by a news bulletin.

"A convicted murderer has escaped from the hospital for the criminally insane. The man was mutilated in a car wreck following a high-speed chase with police, and is missing his right hand. A temporary hook has been attached to his right arm, which will make him easier to identify. The criminal is named..."

The boy turned the radio off. He leaned over to his girlfriend, expecting that the frightening news flash would make her snuggle even closer. Instead, she was so scared that she didn't want to make out any more.

"I'm afraid," she said. "Let's get out of here!"

The boy tried and tried to convince her that they were

in no danger, but she refused to listen. He decided that maybe she didn't like him as much as he had thought, and was just using this as an excuse. The girl reached over and locked her door as the boy angrily started the car.

Just at that moment, they heard a thud on the passenger side of the car!

The boy slammed the car into drive and spun out onto the road. The girl screamed and held onto the boy as they fishtailed around on the road. On the way back to town they both calmed down, but the girl still hung on so tightly that the boyfriend decided he had been wrong about her after all. As they came closer and closer to her house, he tried to think of a way to impress her.

They pulled up in front of her house and the boy said, "I'll make sure it's safe first." He left the keys in the ignition, but locked his door as he got out. He came around to her side to politely open her door, like a hero.

For a long time he just stood there, looking down at her door. At first the girl couldn't figure out what was wrong; then she realized that her door was still locked. She smiled and unlocked it.

The boy still just stood there.

The girl looked puzzled and rolled down her window. Then she saw that the boy was looking down at the door handle. She slowly looked down herself.

A long splatter of blood ran across the door and all the way to the back bumper. Hanging from the door handle was a stainless steel hook.

Pond of Snakes

To intensify the ending scene, this story is often called "The Pond on the Back Forty."

IT WAS A hot summer day and two brothers had finished all their chores on the farm. Their parents were in town in the pickup, and the boys decided to cool off with a swim in the stock pond on the back forty acres of the farm. Their father had always told them not to swim there, to walk a mile down to the creek instead, where it was cooler and the water wasn't dark.

"Don't ever swim in that pond on the back forty," their dad would say. "Go on down to the creek where the water's clear."

But the boys were tired and didn't feel like walking that far; the pickup was in town and the tractor was low on gas. They decided to walk the short distance to the pond. Their dad would never know.

The sun was burning down and the water at the edge of the pond was warm, but the western side of the pond, which

had an earthen dam, was shaded by both the dam and a tree. The muddy, brown water was cool enough there.

The older boy got out of his sweaty overalls quicker, and dove into the murky water while the younger boy was still taking his shoes off. The older boy came up in the shady part of the pond, and shook his head and laughed. Then he dove back under the water with his feet kicking up above the surface of the pond before sinking into the "solid" brown water.

Just as the younger boy was walking into the warm mud at the edge of the pond, getting ready to dive in and cool off, his older brother came out of the water right in the center of the pond. The older boy shot up out of the dark water past his waist.

Sinking back into the water he began to shout. "Go back! Don't come in! Go get Dad!"

The younger brother stood staring at the older boy as he sank back under the brown surface.

"Don't come in!" screamed the older kid. "Go back! Go get Dad!"

And his head disappeared under the water.

The youngster ran as fast as his bare feet would carry him back along the dirt road to the barn. The pickup was just pulling into the yard. The boy raced up to his father and told him what had happened.

"Oh, my God," said the father. "Come on!"

The younger boy, out of breath, had to run hard to keep up with his father. The man ran into the barn and grabbed a grubbing hoe, then tore on down the dirt track to the back forty.

The man began to dig away at the earthen dam that formed the hillside pond, tearing the dirt up with his digging hoe at the lowest point in the dam. The older brother was nowhere in sight.

First, dirty water trickled out of the trench the man was digging, then it began to pour and cut its way through the weakened dam, rushing in snaky, brown waves past the furiously working man. Gradually the flat, silt floor of the pond became visible. There lay the older boy, his body wet and swollen. At first the boy looked like he was starting to move in the now-shallow water. Then the younger brother saw what it was ... crawling across the body of his brother.

A gray water moccasin, the poisonous "cotton-mouthed" snake.

Then another.

Then another.

By the time all the water had drained from the pond, the body of the older boy was covered by hundreds of gray snakes, twisting and rolling, the yellow-and-gray spots on their underbellies flashing in the hot sun.

Hundreds.

The Call from the Downstairs Phone

When being told for shock effect, this story is often called "The Phone Call" or, after a movie based on one version, "When a Stranger Calls."

THE DOCTOR AND his wife were going to a fund-raising banquet and hired a young neighbor to come babysit their two small children. It was the girl's first babysitting job and she was nervous. After the doctor and his wife had left, the girl went upstairs to the children's bedroom. They played for a while and then she read to them. Finally, they both went to sleep. She thought she might go downstairs and sit in the big den to watch TV, but decided to sit in the parents' bedroom next door to the children and read one of the lady's romance novels—something the doctor's wife had suggested, to keep the girl near the children.

After she had read for about an hour, the phone in the

parents' bedroom rang. The girl answered. For a moment there was nothing but silence on the other end of the line. Then a faint voice said, "Get out ... I'm coming to kill the children ... the doctor killed my child ... I'm coming to kill *his* ... get out."

The girl thought it was her boyfriend playing a prank.

"Stop it, Billy," she yelled over the phone. "I know it's you! You're just trying to scare me. Stop it!" She hung up. She didn't think much about it at first, but after about half an hour, the phone rang again.

The babysitter answered slowly, "Hello?"

"Get out of the house ... I'm coming to kill the children ... get out..."

"This isn't funny, Billy!" yelled the girl. Then she whispered when she heard one of the children cry out in her sleep. "Stop it! You're scaring me!"

The caller hung up.

The babysitter went into the next room and adjusted the covers on the children. She was beginning to get really scared. She sat in the dark in the children's bedroom. Seven minutes later, the phone rang again.

"Get out ... I'm coming to kill..."

The babysitter slammed the phone down.

She ran into the children's bedroom and gathered the two sleepy kids into their robes and slippers. She led them to the top of the stairs. The three were just starting down the stairs into the dark lower floor. Three-and-one-half minutes after the last call, the upstairs phone began to ring again.

Slowly, the girl led the children into their parents' bedroom and answered the phone.

"Get out..."

She slammed the receiver down, then picked it up and dialed 911. When the officer answered, she told him that someone had been making threatening phone calls.

"Stay where you are and we'll send a police car to your address."

"I'm not at home," the babysitter said.

The officer laughed and told her the address of the doctor's house. "And let's see," he added, "you're upstairs."

"How did you know that?" whispered the girl hoarsely.

"The computer says that the doctor has a business phone downstairs to take calls from his patients, and a family phone with a different number upstairs. Your call came in on the line from the..."

"The *upstairs* phone," whispered the girl.

Downstairs, something fell over as someone moved slowly in the dark.

The calls were coming from the downstairs phone.

The babysitter dropped the phone and ran to the bedroom door. The door from the parents' room to the children's room had a lock. She locked it.

There were heavy footsteps on the lower stairs.

The girl dragged a chair to the hall door and jammed it under the knob. The knob began to turn from the hall side and someone pushed against the door. It didn't move.

She grabbed the children and they ran to the window. She opened the window and the three climbed out onto the steep roof. Inside, the parents' bedroom door crashed inward.

She and the two children slid dangerously close to the edge of the roof as a man with a butcher knife began climbing out the window onto the roof.

29

As the babysitter hit the edge of the roof, she almost fell off. Her feet dangled over the edge. Something grabbed her feet!

A policeman pulled her and the children off into his arms, and they ran to the waiting police car at the curb.

The Call from the Grave

*This story has both scary and comforting versions. This is
the comforting version.*

ONE TIME THERE was a little girl whose grandfather
had just died. She had loved her grandfather very much and
she missed him a great deal. He was buried in the cemetery
just a few hundred yards from her house, and she could see
his grave every evening at sunset when she looked from her
bedroom window.

One night her parents were going out and the babysitter
hadn't arrived yet. They knew she was a very reliable
babysitter who would probably arrive just a few minutes
later, so they kissed the girl goodbye and drove off.

Hours passed and the babysitter had not yet come. The
girl began to be afraid.

A storm was brewing outside and thunder and lightning
moved closer and closer to the house. Suddenly there was a
bright flash of lightning without any sound and the power in
the house went off. The wind blew the trees around and

branches broke off, crashing against the house and falling to the yard. Alone in the dark, the girl became very scared.

Then the phone rang. Just once.

The girl went to the phone, hoping it was her parents. She said hello, and waited. The line seemed dead. Then, sounding far, far away, a voice came over the phone.

It was her grandfather's voice.

"Don't be afraid, honey. There's nothing to fear. You'll be safe in the house. The storm will pass over."

Then the phone was silent and dead.

The girl went to bed, calm and happy. She slept well in spite of the rain.

The parents came home and found their daughter asleep, and, unwilling to wake her, they left their questions until the morning. They were horrified when the babysitter called the next morning to explain that she had been in a wreck at the leading edge of the storm. She was unhurt, but what had their daughter done alone in the house?

When they woke her, she told them what had happened. And when they didn't believe her, she smiled and pointed out her window to what she had seen the night before.

The phone line from the house was intact out to the first phone pole, but then it was broken by fallen limbs, and the cable drooped into the cemetery.

The end of the broken line lay across her grandfather's grave.

Last Kiss

This is perhaps the oldest urban legend, and has hundreds of versions with many different titles, including "The Vanishing Hitchhiker."

LATE ONE NIGHT a young man was driving home along a dark country road. It was Saturday night and it was raining. As he rounded a long curve, his headlights lit up a young woman standing at the side of the road. She was wearing a white dress and was all wet from the rain. He thought he knew what had happened: the girl had quarreled with her date and had chosen to walk home rather than stay with the guy. The young man skidded to a stop before the young woman even raised her hand to thumb a ride.

He leaned over and opened the door for her to get in.

She slid into the seat and shut the door. With a smile she said, "Would you take me home? I just live a mile down the road."

That was when he noticed how really pretty she was. He almost couldn't think of anything to say, she was so pretty.

He said, "Sure," or something like that, and took off his letter jacket and offered it to her. She leaned forward and he draped it around her shoulders. It was too crowded in the front seat for her to put her arms into the sleeves.

The boy dropped the car into gear, and he still hadn't really thought of anything to say when they passed the church and the graveyard and came to a two-story house.

"This is my house," she said.

They stopped, and he got out and walked her to the door. They stood looking at each other for a moment and before he could think of a way to ask for a kiss, she leaned over and kissed him! He was so surprised that she had opened the screen door, opened the front door, and gone inside the house before he could speak. He realized that she was still wearing his letter jacket and for a moment he thought about knocking on the door. But the house was dark, her parents were probably asleep, and she might get into trouble for coming in so late if he woke them.

Besides, the jacket gave him the perfect excuse to see her again!

Sunday morning, about time for church, he came back to the house and knocked on the door. A tired, sad-looking woman answered. He asked if he could talk to the lady's daughter.

"My daughter is dead," said the woman. "She died one year ago last night, in a car wreck down the road a mile or so at the long curve."

"That's not possible," said the young man. "I gave her a ride home last night!"

"If you don't believe me," said the woman, "go look for yourself. She's buried in the graveyard there, in the third row."

The young man walked into the cemetery. In the third row of headstones, he found what he was looking for.

A pink marble headstone was inscribed with the name *Laurie,* and over the rounded corners of the stone was his letter jacket.

THE URBAN RUNNERS-UP

These next six frightening urban legends are the runners-up in the favorite scary stories contest. Each one has dozens of versions or variants all across the country, but this is the way we've most often heard and told them.

Outside the Door

This story has other names, including "The Girl Outside the Door."

IT WAS THE holidays and most of the kids had gone home from boarding school for a week. Some of the students, however, lived too far away, or their parents were out of the country, or someone was coming to pick them up later in the week. To save electricity and heating oil, all the students from all the dorms were moved into two dorms temporarily, one for guys and one for gals.

In the girls' dorm, two girls who had never met were put into a room together. They hit it off well from the first, and the sun had long set when they got back from the dining commons that night and went to their room.

The older girl told the younger girl that she had seen someone in the shadows outside the dorm, and they agreed to keep the door to the room locked. Then the older girl went down the hall to take a shower.

She was gone a long time and the younger girl began to

get scared. She stood with her ear against the locked door of the room, hoping to hear the older girl coming down the hall. What she heard terrified her.

It was a noise like a huge snake, sliding down the hall and moving slowly toward the door. Then she heard a gurgling sound, like a monster blowing bubbles in the water of a lagoon. Then something began to claw at the door, scratching as if it wanted to get in.

The younger girl screamed.

What *was* that thing outside the room—some kind of huge, hideous animal that crawled like a snake and clawed at the door? The scratching went on and on! Was it some kind of maniac? What weapon did he have? Was he cutting slowly through the door?

The younger girl retreated from the door into a corner away from the windows. She slid slowly down into a seated position and began to cry. The scratching, clawing sound went on.

For hours.

The girl cried herself to sleep.

When she woke up, it was bright outside, long after sunrise. There was no sound at all in the dorm. There was no sound at all in the hall. The younger girl walked slowly to the door.

Did she dare to open it?

She gently took hold of the knob with one hand.

Was the monster waiting just outside, waiting for her to open the door?

She took the knob of the door lock in the other hand.

Was the maniac just down the hall with his weapon, waiting?

Slowly she turned the lock.

Slowly she turned the knob.

Slowly she opened the door.

On the hall floor was the other girl, dead in a pool of blood. Her throat had been cut. The door was covered with scratches from her fingernails. She had been trying to get the younger girl to let her in.

The Killer in the Back Seat

When told for shock effect, this story is often called "In the Rear-View Mirror."

A LADY WAS driving alone across country. She stopped for a cup of coffee at a dingy old café out in the middle of nowhere. She was a little scared to go in alone, but there were a lot of cars and several semis parked outside, so she knew there would be some safety in numbers. Inside, she had a donut and coffee, and was feeling fairly safe until she spotted a greasy-looking guy with a beard who was watching her very closely from across the room.

Soon she couldn't take her eyes off him, for fear he might move closer to her without her seeing. She ate quickly and got up to leave. He got up too.

She hurried to the cash register and bumped into a man in a plaid shirt on the way out. The bearded guy came out only seconds later. She stepped around behind a large sign, hoping to lose him, but when she peeked out, she saw him standing at the edge of the parking lot, looking toward her car. She looked around for the man in the plaid shirt to ask for help, but didn't see him anywhere.

As she ran from the sign to her car she saw the man with the beard running parallel to her, then getting into a semi. She quickly got into her car, and as she roared out onto the road, she could see the semi in the rear-view mirror, pulling onto the road behind her.

She sped up, but the truck slowly gained on her during the downhill stretches. She changed lanes and even turned onto another highway, hoping the semi wouldn't follow her.

Yet there it was in the rear-view mirror. The truck came closer and closer to her rear bumper.

The bearded man began to honk the horn and flash the truck lights up and down. The lady was terrified. No matter what she did, the truck stayed right behind her.

Ahead, she saw a rest area with bright lights and lots of parked cars. She swerved across the lanes and took the off-ramp into the rest area. The truck swerved after her, its tires squealing. She pulled into the passenger car parking area and the semi followed her into the narrow lane.

The lady skidded to a stop and got out. She started running toward the restrooms, where there were a lot of people standing and staring at her.

The bearded man jumped from the cab of the semi, carrying his tire-checking bat, and he ran—straight to the lady's car.

Suddenly, out of the backseat of her car came the man in the plaid shirt! He was carrying a huge hunting knife.

The bearded truck driver hit the knife-wielding man and

knocked him out. The people at the rest area ran over to help hold the man in the plaid shirt for the police.

The bearded truck driver walked slowly across the grass to the lady and smiled. "Couldn't you see that guy," he asked, "in your rear-view mirror?"

The Little White Dog

*Every time this story is told, someone says, "I know that story, only when **I** heard it..."*

THE**RE WAS AN** old woman who had no family still living. Her only friend was a little white dog who went everywhere with her—with one exception. The dog loved the fireplace in winter, and after the old woman went to bed he would sometimes go and lie in front of the warm coals. Usually, though, the dog slept at the very edge of the bed on a throw rug.

The woman wouldn't allow the dog on the bed with her, but if she became frightened or had a nightmare, she would put her hand down to the little white dog and he would lick it reassuringly.

One night the woman was reading her newspaper just before going to sleep. She shivered and pulled the comforter up around her as she read that a mental patient had wandered off from a nearby hospital. No one knew if the patient was dangerous or not; he was a suspect in the

murders of several women who had lived alone.

The woman turned out the lights and tried to sleep, but she was frightened, and tossed and turned fitfully. Finally, she reached down to where the little white dog slept. Sure enough, a warm, wet tongue began to lick her hand. The woman felt reassured and safe, and left her hand dangling off the bed as she turned and settled in comfortably. She opened her eyes for a moment and looked through the open door into the living room.

There, in front of the fireplace, sat her little white dog, gazing at the coals and wagging his tail.

And down beside the bed something was still licking her hand.

Step-Drag

There are hundreds of versions of this classic summer camp scary story. This one supposedly happened in Virginia.

THIS WAS THE hottest summer anyone could remember at the Big Pines Camp up in the mountains. It was between sessions: three busloads of younger children had just left and three busloads of new ones wouldn't arrive until Monday at noon. That left the five young camp counselors alone for a peaceful weekend.

Unknown to them, another bus—a gray prison bus—was winding along the mountain roads, transporting a single prisoner. The man was criminally insane, according to the tag on his prison uniform, and the two guards assigned to him believed it. He was very tall and strong, so his hands were manacled in huge handcuffs and his legs were hobbled close to each other with a chain. To keep him from running or kicking out at anyone, the warden had added an old-fashioned ball-and-chain, which he'd found in a prison storeroom. That kind of thing hadn't been used since the 1920s. The chain was clamped to the maniac's right ankle, and the heavy iron ball was on the end of the two-foot chain.

The maniac was sitting quietly with his eyes closed, smiling that same simple smile he always smiled just to keep the guards wondering. Thinking that the maniac was asleep, the guards weren't being watchful enough. As the bus swerved on a tight mountain curve, one guard slid off the wooden bench and fell against the prisoner, who wasn't asleep at all. He quickly grabbed the guard by the neck with the short chain on his handcuffs.

While they struggled, the other guard got up and went after the maniac. The prisoner dropped the strangled guard and lunged at the other one. The guard tried to draw his pistol, but the maniac had picked up the iron ball and thrown it before the guard had so much as a chance.

The maniac found keys on the guards to remove the cuffs and the leg irons, but he couldn't find a key for the ball-and-chain. He picked up the iron ball again, smashed the wire-glass window to the cab of the prison bus, and grabbed the driver by the throat. The bus swerved all over the mountain road and finally went over an embankment. It crashed into a tree and the side walls of the bus caved in. The maniac was out!

Back at the camp, the counselors had swum all afternoon and were now back in their cabins reading or listening to the radio. There wasn't a TV anywhere in the camp. The sun went down and the owls began to hoot scarily off in the distance. Suddenly someone screamed! Everyone came running out of their cabins and met at the assembly ground.

Missy was missing! The other four ran to her cabin. The door was standing open and there was a pool of blood on the floor. The counselors gasped, then suddenly became very quiet.

"Ssshhh!" whispered Jamey. They all strained to listen. In the trees, somewhere nearby, they could hear:

Step ... drag ... step ... drag ... step ... drag...

"Let's split up and look for her!" said Destiny. They all ran off in different directions into the dark woods. After a few minutes Jamey yelled for everyone to come to him. It was hard to follow his voice in the underbrush; it was hard to believe that the woods so near the camp were this thick and impenetrable. Soon Destiny and Tiffany found Jamey staring up into a tree. There, in the moonlight, was Todd. He was hanging by his head in a fork of the tree branches; his neck must have been broken.

Off to the south they could hear noises in the undergrowth:

Step ... drag ... step ... drag ... step ... drag...

Jamey climbed the tree and lowered the body to the girls. The three of them carried the limp corpse back to the mess hall. Once inside, the girls started crying and Jamey hurried to lock all the doors with the big wooden bars.

"You girls stay here," he said, "and lock this door behind me. I've got to get to the main building where the phone is."

The girls objected, but Jamey went out the front door and slipped off in the darkness. The girls dropped the bar back into its metal brackets, to prevent anyone from entering. After a few minutes the lights suddenly went out. The girls started to scream, but then they realized that whoever had cut the wires might not know where they were. They held their hands over their mouths and hid under the serving counter.

Suddenly, something rattled the front door. It must be the maniac! The girls huddled together. Next they heard something outside the window just above them, something dragging along the ground, going:

Step ... drag ... step ... drag ... step ... drag...

The double doors rattled again. Jamey whispered, "Hey, let me in!" The dragging sound was moving around the building going toward the back door. Jamey gasped louder, "Let me in!"

Tiffany ran from the counter to the door and lifted the bar. Jamey darted into the dark mess hall like a scared cat.

Just as they got the double doors shut, the dragging sound came around to the front. Just as they dropped the wooden bar into its brackets, something huge and heavy hit the door, cracking the wood.

Jamey and Tiffany ran across the room, tripping and stumbling over chairs in the dark. The object hit the door again, and the wooden bar cracked with a loud noise. The two counselors looked under the serving counter. Destiny wasn't there! They ran to the back door.

"The phone lines must have been cut," whispered Jamey. "The phone was dead." The heavy weight hit the front door again, breaking part of the door's upper half. Jamey and Tiffany lifted the bar from the back door and swung it open. Another crash at the front door told them the doors were about to give. The two slipped into the tall pantry and closed the door.

Back in the mess hall, the double front doors gave way in a burst of splinters and broken boards. A deathly silence followed. The two counselors hardly dared to breathe. Suddenly, they heard that sound out on the wooden floor:

Step ... drag ... step ... drag ... step ... drag...

The sound stopped right outside the pantry door. Tiffany gasped. Jamey cupped his hand over her mouth and the two held their breath. Jamey was afraid the thing outside could hear his heart beating.

Suddenly there was a terrible scream outside the pantry.

It was Destiny! She had moved to another hiding place, leaving Tiffany and Jamey on their own. Now the thing, whatever it was, had found her. There was another scream and the sound of something going out the open back door.

Then everything was as quiet as a graveyard.

The two waited all night, hardly breathing. The sun began to come up; they could see light coming in through the cracks of the wooden pantry. A mourning dove was calling softly in the woods.

Then they heard a sound. Someone was coming in the front door. Slow footsteps crossed the floor, along with the sound of something dragging along the boards.

The sound came closer to the pantry.

Closer.

Suddenly it stopped, right in front of the pantry door, as if someone was waiting.

Tiffany couldn't stand it anymore. She screamed.

The pantry door swung open, and there standing over them was a tall, muscular form, lit from behind. The man bent over.

He took off his wide-brimmed hat and showed them his badge. "I'm the sheriff," he said, dropping the heavy bag of weapons and bulletproof vests he had been dragging. "Thank God you two are all right!"

The Lady from the Lake

This is a variant of "The Vanishing Hitchhiker." See what Dr. Brunvand says in the Introduction.

THERE WAS A full moon and the lake was calm and clear. The car moved slowly along Lake Shore Drive, headed for the state park. Suddenly, the driver saw a figure in the trees beside the road on the lake side. As the car drew closer, a young woman dressed in white stepped out onto the pavement. She was dripping wet, as if she had been swimming, and had put on a thin, white gauze cover-up over her swimsuit. At first the driver thought she had been about to cross the road, perhaps headed for a campsite or a cabin. But she was standing there now as if she were waiting for him to stop.

The young man stopped, introduced himself as Isaac, and offered her a ride. She thanked him and got in. She apologized for being wet, but Isaac told her the seat covers were vinyl and not to worry.

"Been swimming kind of late, haven't you?" asked Isaac.

"I love the lake by moonlight," said the girl in white, without introducing herself or answering his question.

"Where can I take you?" asked the boy.

"Right up there," she said, pointing to a condominium complex.

He let her out where she indicated. She thanked him, still without introducing herself, and disappeared into the lobby.

The next day Isaac went back to the condo, hoping to see the girl at the pool or somewhere on the grounds. But he never found her, so he went to the desk to try to learn who she was. No one in the condo recognized his description of her. Finally he gave up and went downtown to the library, where he was researching a school paper about the impact of the nearby dam and lake on the environment. As he looked through the microfilms of ten-year-old newspapers, he saw something that made his blood run cold.

It was her! The lady from the lake. Her picture was on the front page of a newspaper dated exactly ten years ago that day. The headline said simply, *Local Girl Missing. Car Runs Off Uncompleted Dam.*

The Headless Brakeman

This story is told about many different places, but the most famous versions come from the area of Gurdon and Crossett, Arkansas.

BEFORE 1970, FREIGHT trains always had a caboose as the last car. In the caboose there were a table and some chairs, supplies and equipment for the brakeman, and sometimes even a bunk bed so that two brakemen could work and sleep in shifts. Some cabooses also had a stove for cooking meals while the train was moving. The brakeman stood on the back platform of the caboose as the train went over trestles, through tunnels or intersections, and as the train was coming into a station. He watched for trouble; he used his lantern when it was dark to signal to the engineer, and he could apply the safety brakes to help stop the train if there was trouble.

When the train was in the station or stopped for loading or unloading at a sawmill or gravel plant, the brakeman would walk along the stopped train checking the couplings that held the cars together. At night he would carry a lantern to see the couplings and to signal to the engineer.

One night years ago, a long freight train came to a stop on the tracks outside Crossett. Something was wrong; the train wasn't moving the way it should. The brakeman got out with his lantern to check the couplings. He got about halfway from the caboose to the engine and thought he saw something wrong.

He leaned into the space between the freight cars and looked down at the heavy metal grips that interlocked to fasten the cars together, the same way a man locks his fists together with his fingers. While the brakeman was bent over he carelessly reached down between the couplings, which had not been fastened together properly back in the railroad yard.

Just then, the old steam engine moved just a little, because the brakes that were supposed to hold it still were old and worn. The engine moved about six inches along the track and all the cars jerked and lurched as the forward movement worked its way back through the train like a caterpillar wiggling. The car in front of the brakeman moved forward and the safety chain that connected it to the car behind the brakeman pulled the back car forward. The brakeman was knocked off his feet and he dropped his lantern. When he fell, his head passed between the metal grips as the coupling slammed closed.

The cars were coupled together firmly now and the brakeman's blood dripped off the coupling. His body lay alongside the track. His lantern lay to the side.

His head lay on the tracks, between the cars.

The fireman and the engineer saw the lantern fall and ran back to the headless body. They put the body in the caboose, but neither of them could find the head when they went back to look for it.

To this day, the ghost of the brakeman walks slowly up and down the track at night, carrying a ghostly, dim lantern.

Looking for his lost head.

A TERROR TOUR
OF OUR NATION

The Midwest is the region of the United States that is "home" to the greatest number of scary legends, but the stories are popular all over North America. Join us now on a terror tour, from the New England coast around the nation, past Mexico, up the Pacific coast to Alaska and over Canada to the American heartland. These scary stories rule from sea to shining sea.

The Wendigo

This story hails from Southeastern Canada, Maine, Vermont, and New Hampshire.

DEEP IN THE North Woods of New England two hunters were out to break the law and bag a moose. They had tracked the moose all day in the snow and were hoping to catch him in a clearing, where an easy shot might bring him down. But the sun went down—fast, as it does in autumn—and the two hunters pitched a quick camp in a wooded area where the snow was lightly dusted across the carpet of pine needles on the ground.

After darkness set in and the fire burned low, one man went to sleep. The other stayed awake watching the fire and thinking about nothing in particular. Suddenly, a distant voice called his name.

He sat bolt upright and looked into the darkness. After a moment, he decided it was only night voices—those faraway sounds that your mind thinks are words when you have sat for hours without hearing any words. One other thought did cross his mind...

Again, somehow closer, and high in the sky, he heard something call his name.

It had to be his imagination; it couldn't possibly be ... the Wendigo. The Indians believed there was a spirit woman who lived in the sky, flew on the wind, and protected the forest and its inhabitants. She would call out to a hapless wrong-doer until she had him in her spell. Then she would lead him by the hand, or grasp him by the hair, as she floated above him. As they traveled faster and faster, the man's feet would run along the ground so hard that they would catch fire! At last the Wendigo would lift the victim off the ground and either carry him away into the sky to eat him for dinner, or let him drop to the land below. But the hunter knew that was impossible.

Again, closer to the tent, something called his name.

He tried with all his strength to resist. He covered his ears with his hands. He screamed for his buddy to wake up. The other man slept on, unhearing, and the voice came closer.

Closer.

Closer.

Suddenly, the other hunter, a man named Caleb, awoke from a deep sleep. He jumped up and came outside the tent, wondering what he had heard that awoke him. In the distance he heard his buddy scream.

"My feet ... my feet ... my burning feet!"

Caleb began to run, following his buddy's tracks in the patchy snow. The screaming continued, getting farther and farther away. He ran as fast as he could. Where the snow ran out he found footprints in the pine needles.

Smoking footprints.

The prints were getting further and further apart, and soon the prints were tiny circles of burning pine and fir needles. The screams drifted across the night sky with the wind and were gone.

Caleb ran to the place where the last footprint burned, still in its boot-sole shape. The snow beyond was trackless, like the sky. He stood for several minutes, staring up, shivering violently from the cold and the fear. Suddenly, he saw something resembling a bird high in the sky. It was like an eagle, swooping down on its prey. The dark silhouette came closer and closer, growing larger and larger. Caleb was frozen in fear, his mouth wide open in a scream, as the dark shape rushed toward him, becoming identifiable as it plummeted to earth.

It was the lifeless body of the other hunter.

It hammered into the snow and earth as it hit, creating a hideous "snow angel" right in front of Caleb. His buddy's eyes were wide and staring, seeing nothing. His mouth was open wide, saying nothing. And his legs ended too soon—in smoking, dripping stumps without boots, without feet. Steam rose from the snow around the charred, bloody stumps.

Caleb staggered out of the woods the next morning and told his friends of a small forest fire, started due to his buddy's carelessness at the campfire, that took his partner's feet and his life.

And he never hunted in those woods again.

Tad O'Cain
and the Corpse

This comes from Massachusetts, New York, Pennsylva-
nia, and anywhere that Irish-Americans live and remember
the old stories.

TAD O'CAIN WAS the youngest son of a rich man, and
his father loved him best. The boy grew up spoiled, always
getting everything he asked for from his father. As he grew
older, he drank and gambled and spent all his nights in the
local pubs with the dancing girls. His fellow townspeople
predicted that when the father died the youngest son would
inherit everything, and lose it all in a year.

Finally, the father saw what he had done by spoiling his
son. He wanted to make it right, but didn't know how. He
tried the only thing he could think of—he told Tad that he
must settle down, end his riotous life, and marry one of the
local girls.

Tad was furious! He stormed out of the great old house and walked for hours along the road, smoking his pipe and trying to get rid of his anger. He cursed and swore as he walked along, and ended up saying out loud, "I'd as soon dance with a dead man as get married before I'm ready!"

Just then the great bell in the church tower far behind him tolled midnight.

As Tad walked by the little empty chapel in the woods and past its small, old graveyard, he heard voices. A low fog rolled over the road, and in it walked about twenty little, gnarled, black creatures. They were carrying something heavy, which they set down on the road in front of Tad.

It was a rotten corpse, stiff in mummification, with hollow eye sockets staring and mouth agape. Its arms were folded over its chest, and rags of clothing and rotten flesh hung loose from it.

Tad's blood went cold and he stood frozen in fear. One of the little creatures stepped out of the fog and greeted him.

"Now, isn't it lucky that we met you just now?" said the wrinkled little thing.

Tad was too terrified to speak.

"Isn't it just in time that we came along?" asked the little creature with a twinkle in its red eye.

Tad trembled and his jaw shook but he couldn't say a thing.

"Now, isn't it lucky and just in time that we've met?" the black shape repeated. Tad shook as the little thing looked him up and down. "You've got your wish, Tad O'Cain," said the creature, lifting a bony claw and pointing to the corpse. "Get up," it said to the corpse.

The dead, rotten thing stood slowly and stiffly and

turned its hollow eyes to Tad. He quickly decided to flee as the dead man stepped slowly toward him. Tad managed to get turned around to run, but the dead man grabbed him about the chest with his rotten arms and clung to him like someone riding piggyback.

"Now," said the little black creature, "it's your duty to take this poor soul and bury him. He has been lying in an unmarked spot for a year now and deserves better. Get you to a church and bury him, and if you are denied entrance at any church, go on to the next, until you have it done. You have until sunrise. Now, be gone with you!"

The black creatures in the fog laughed, howled, clicked their tongues, and came running out of the fog chasing Tad. Suddenly Tad found he could move, and move he did, as fast as he could, down the road with the dead man on his back.

At the old gray church, Tad went through the gate and tried the huge wooden door. It was locked.

"The key ... is above ... the door," said the corpse on Tad's back, and Tad let out a scream. He reached above the door and found the key. In this church the dead were buried under the stones of the church floor. Tad found a spade in the corner of the church, but when he lifted a stone from the floor and drove the shovel into the ground, a dead hand came up and pushed the shovel aside. When he lifted another stone and dug, a corpse sat up out of the dirt and pushed him away, pulling the stone back down over itself like a man pulling the covers over him in bed. The third place he dug, a horribly rotten old woman sat up in a broken coffin and reached for Tad's throat. He screamed and dropped the stone back over her.

"I can't bury you here. The ground's all full!" Tad

cried, and ran out the door with the dead thing on his back.

He staggered down the road, lost, and the right arm of the corpse let go of him long enough to point the way at a crossroads. Again and again the dead man pointed the way until Tad arrived at a second chapel and burying ground. He stumbled through the gate and into the cemetery, but as he walked in, a white ghost rose out of a grave and blocked his way. Every way he turned, dozens of spirits shot up out of their graves, blocking his path. At last there were hundreds.

"I can't bury you here," he cried. "These are all honest churchgoers, and they'll not admit the likes of you *or* me!" Tad turned and staggered out onto the road.

The corpse pointed again and again, as Tad stumbled on under the weight. Tad fell down over and over again, and was bruised and bleeding as he reached the third church. The graveyard was surrounded by a low, broken-down wall. There was no longer a church here—just a burying ground. There were almost no stone markers and the graveyard was in terrible disrepair, with weeds and saplings growing among the graves.

The first glow of dawn was forming in the east; Tad was running out of time. He stumbled into the graveyard and almost fell into an open, fresh grave. At the bottom of the hole was a black coffin with its lid open. The coffin was empty.

As Tad stood over the grave, reeling and swaying from pain and exhaustion, the corpse on his back gave a huge sigh. A cloud of stinking, dusty air came out of the dead man's mouth. It relaxed its grip on Tad and fell off. Tad stepped aside and the corpse slid neatly into the hole, dropped into the coffin, and fell out lengthwise in it. The lid closed with a slam just as the sun was beginning to rise.

Tad slowly filled the hole, scooping the fresh dirt with his cupped hands until the grave was finished. Then he staggered to a nearby inn and rented a room. He slept all day and all night, and went home the next day ragged and bruised.

He gave up drink and gambling and married one of the pretty dancing girls from his former favorite pub. They lived happy all their lives.

But Tad O'Cain never stayed out until midnight again.

Phantom Ship

This scary story comes from Connecticut and Rhode Island.

THERE IS A long island that stretches east from New York City. The island protects many cities and harbors from the storms of the North Atlantic Ocean. Across from the part of the island called South End Point lies the safe harbor of New Haven, Connecticut. On a very quiet night, under a full moon, as clouds roll in from the sea, some people say they see a ghostly ship sailing above the water, coming home ... again.

The story begins a long time ago, before the states were united together into one nation. All the cities of the east coast were in colonies of Great Britain. In order to send trade goods and passengers back to England, a company of businessmen hired a great sailing ship to make the trip. The leader of the company was George Lamberton, and he was named captain of the ship for this voyage.

The ship sailed into New Haven from Rhode Island. It

was a wide ship with tall masts and great canvas sails, but some sailors looked at it and said it was clumsy in the water, as if it were built poorly. The ship was loaded with cargo and passengers and prepared to set sail.

It was winter, and all the people of the town of New Haven went out to bid farewell to the ship and her passengers. They walked along the ice, waving, as the ship sailed out the narrow passageway through the ice. The great ship had a fine name, the *Fellowship*.

Months passed and the *Fellowship* did not return from its long voyage. Others ships came from Britain and said the *Fellowship* had not yet landed when they had sailed. After eight months, the people of New Haven knew what must have happened. The *Fellowship* had been lost at sea, perhaps sunk in a storm. All that summer people who had lost friends or relatives on the *Fellowship* would sit by the sea and watch to see if the great ship was coming home.

Then, in June of 1648, a summer storm blew in from the Atlantic. Huge, high clouds led the storm as it came toward the harbor. In the orange light from the sunset in the west, as it reflected off the huge clouds, the *Fellowship* began to appear. The great ship moved slowly out of the cloud bank, riding the air, above the level of the actual harbor. Hundreds of people saw it and ran from their houses and shops to the harbor as the flying ship came in.

The ship came so close that people could see the captain standing on the bow with his sword raised. People ran to touch the ship. Then it began to break up. The masts snapped silently and toppled forward. The sails fell over parts of the ship, covering them with white canvas, like the white clouds. The ship began to sink toward the sea, and into the rolling wall of clouds. Soon the clouds hit the shore and the cold wind drove all the people back to their homes. Only the cold fog remained.

This must have been how the *Fellowship* looked as it sank in a storm. And now the ship must have come home to end the fears of the people of New Haven. Knowing the sad truth was better than always wondering what had happened.

Some nights, as a storm blows in at sunset, some of the people of New Haven say they see the *Fellowship* again, high in the clouds—a phantom ship.

Spin! Spin! Reel Off, Skin!

From the Carolinas, Georgia, Alabama, Mississippi, and Louisiana comes this supernatural tale.

IN THE LOW country of the Carolinas, all the folks know of and fear the evil women called boo-hags. Sometimes someone you love turns out to be a boo-hag. There are several ways to protect your home against a boo-hag and her evil lover, a boo-daddy, but the best way is to paint your window frames and door frames blue.

One night a young man who had just married a lovely young woman who was new in the town heard a noise in the attic. When he got up to see what was wrong he saw that his new bride was not in bed. He searched the house, but couldn't find her anywhere. He went up into the attic and saw a small doorway in one wall, in a gable in the roof. It was a door used in olden times to raise furniture or trunks

directly to and from the attic, without having to climb stairs or use a ladder. As he looked at the open door swinging in the breeze, he noticed something.

The door frame wasn't painted blue.

He went back to bed worried, but he fell asleep anyway because he had worked hard that day in the cane field.

The next morning his bride was asleep in the bed when he awoke. He said nothing about the night before.

That evening, after supper, the young man yawned and pretended to be very tired. (Actually he had told the foreman he was feeling bad—he was, about his wife—and had slept all afternoon under a tree without pay.) Nevertheless, he went upstairs to bed early and pretended to be asleep.

His bride came in later and lay down. He pretended to snore. As soon as she was sure he was asleep, the young woman got up and went back downstairs. She took off her nightgown and sat naked at her old ashwood spinning wheel. She put her foot on the treadle and began to pump it up and down. The wheel began to spin and the spindle— where the yarn would wind up—began to turn.

The young woman pulled on one of her fingers as if she were taking off a glove ... and her skin came loose!

She touched her loose-skinned finger to the spindle and the skin began to wrap around the spindle like yarn.

She began to sing, "Spin! Spin! Reel off, skin!"

And her skin slid off her hand, off her arm, off her whole body and wrapped itself around the spindle in a tight, bloody blob. The woman who sat on the spinning stool was now a bloody, red, fleshless thing. Her eyes had no lids and stared like the eyes in a skinned pig's head at the market. Her body was all red muscle and white sinew, like a butchered side of beef. She was a boo-hag!

The husband, who had snuck downstairs and watched it all from behind a door, gasped in fear.

The hag turned and looked about. The young man froze in terror, holding his breath. The hag laughed a hideous, growling laugh. The young man, in his stocking feet, stayed a few steps ahead of the hag as he ran quietly back to bed. The hag looked in on him, but the young man was snoring quietly as if he were asleep.

The hag climbed the ladder like an animal and went into the attic by the trapdoor. The husband followed and watched as the bloody hag launched herself out the door. She stretched out her arms and soared like a huge, ghastly bird. After circling over the house and laughing a horrible laugh, she rose out of sight to meet her boo-daddy, the real love of her life, somewhere above the swamp.

As she flew over the town, milk soured in the milk pans in the houses below, people's old wounds began to bleed again, and cats turned mean and tried to kill their masters.

The young man knelt at the attic door and cried for a moment over the loss of his wife. He knew what he had to do. He went out to the shed and got the blue paint. He painted the frame around the attic door in the moonlight, then he shut it and latched it from the inside.

Back downstairs, he went to the spinning wheel and unreeled the long, thin sack of skin from the spindle. He took it to the kitchen and got down the salt and pepper shakers from the cupboard. He poured the salt and all the pepper into the skin-sack and shook it up to coat the bloody inside. Then he hung the skin on a nail outside the back door on the porch.

He went inside and sat at the kitchen table, with elbows

on the table and his head in his hands. By dawn the lamp had burned low and he again heard the horrid laughter in the sky.

The boo-hag flew to the attic door and screamed like a mountain lion when she saw the blue paint. She flew down and around and around the house, looking for a way in. Then she saw her skin hanging on the nail.

She whooshed down onto the porch and crouched like a vicious animal, looking around for her human husband in order to kill him. But he was inside, waiting, knowing what would come next.

The boo-hag sniffed her skin, but she couldn't smell the salt and pepper deep inside it. She lifted the skin-sack and began to put it on. She had just pulled her face over her bloody skull and was almost human-looking again, when she felt the salt and pepper.

The hag let out a scream like an animal trapped in a fire!

She shook and she squirmed and she spun and she screamed. She clawed at her skin and tore it to rags. Blood poured out of her flesh and ran across the floorboards of the porch. She spun around again and threw out her arms. She flew up into the air, twirling and whirling, and out over the swamp.

She spun faster and faster, trying to stop the burning, until she burst into a thousand pieces of bloody red meat and bone. The pieces fell like rain into the swamp.

The alligators ate well that morning.

Tailbones

Coming from the Virginias, Kentucky, Tennessee, Arkansas, and Missouri, this story has other names like "Tailybones" or "Tailypo" and other versions like "Chunk O' Meat." It is based on the motif called "Golden Arm." A Hispanic version called "Give Me Back My Guts!" is found on page 149.

ONCE THERE WAS an old man hunting in the woods with his dogs. He hunted for all his meat, but he hadn't had any luck for several days. He had been eating nothing but turnips and was ready for some meat for a change.

He said to himself, "Today, no matter what I catch, I'm going to eat it up!"

Just about then his dogs started barking as if they had seen or smelled a deer or some other large animal. The dogs raced through the underbrush, and the man ran in the direction of the sound of the barking.

Soon the man was right behind his dogs, running through the bushes and brambles, chasing something that he couldn't make out in the trees ahead. They broke into a clearing and the dogs, confused, looked every which way, sniffing the air. Then the dogs all started off in different directions.

"That's odd," said the man to himself.

The dogs should have been able to follow the trail of anything—well, anything natural. The man began looking around and soon found a huge tree with a hole in it where a branch had broken away in a storm, carving out the tree's rotten interior. There was something hanging out of the hole.

Something furry.

Like a huge tail.

But no animal was that big. Nothing natural, anyway.

The man poked at the tail and it twitched a little, yet whatever was hiding deep in that huge, hollow tree didn't move or make a sound. The man pulled on the tail. It swished from side to side, but nothing else happened. The man fired a bullet into the thing and the tail flicked about a little, but still nothing else happened.

Finally, the man said, "Well, meat's meat, and I intend to eat." He took out his hunting knife and cut the tail off right at the tree bark. The tail wriggled and a little blood flowed from the tree, but nothing else happened.

The man called his dogs by blowing on a cowhorn, and they all went home.

That night, after he had fed his dogs some of the meat raw, he skinned the tail and began to cook it. As the meat roasted, he went to the back room of his cabin and began cleaning his gun. Outside he heard the dogs suddenly barking at an animal again.

Then, one by one, the dogs yelped in fear and ran away

into the woods, barking as they went. Something stepped up onto the porch.

"I want my tailbones," said a growly voice outside the cabin.

The man sat perfectly still. The front door creaked open.

"I want my tailbones," said a low, grinding voice.

The man tried to move, but he was paralyzed with fear. Something that sounded like claws dragged across the floor of the main room.

"I want my tailbones," said the deep, hollow, hoarse voice.

The man was sweating blood. His rifle was clean, but unloaded. A noise like teeth grinding and claws tearing the floorboards came closer and closer to the fireplace and the door to the back room.

"I ... WANT ... MY ... TAILBONES!" howled the snarling voice.

"WELL, TAKE THEM!" yelled the man.

Rosewood Casket

This story is from Tennessee, Missouri, Arkansas, Oklahoma, and Texas.

A POOR FAMILY that lived in the hills had several older children and a new little baby. The baby took sick with a high fever. Finally, the baby stopped breathing altogether.

The father went to the attic and took down a beautiful piece of furniture that had been a family heirloom for many generations. It was a table made of rosewood. He took the table apart and fashioned a beautiful little casket—a rosewood casket. The mother cut up her wedding dress, and the white satin and lace she had saved for years to buy was used to line the rosewood casket.

They laid the lifeless baby in the casket and buried her in the family plot in the corner of the high field. That night the mother had a dream.

"John, wake up," she said to her husband. "I dreamed the baby was crying!"

"The baby is gone, Mary," said John sadly. "Go back to sleep."

The next night the woman woke up, more desperate than before.

"John, wake up! I tell you, the baby is crying!"

Again, John reminded her that the baby was gone.

The third night, Mary woke up screaming.

"John, John! The baby is crying! We've got to do something!"

John tried to comfort her, but Mary refused to listen. She put on her housedress and her bonnet and went to the kitchen. She lit a lantern and went to the shed for a shovel. John caught up with her, still fastening the galluses on his overalls. They went toward the family plot, with some of the older kids following in their nightshirts.

John took the shovel and began to dig. When he became winded, the oldest boy took the shovel and kept digging until he reached the rosewood casket. There was no sound as they lifted the casket from the grave.

There was no sound as they pried the nails out of the beautiful rosewood lid.

There was no sound as they sadly lifted the lid to look inside.

The still, pale baby lay surrounded by satin and lace. Then, very faintly, there was a sound.

The baby opened her eyes and began to cry.

Angelina

In southern Arizona there is a legend about a light in a blizzard; this kind of story is found throughout the United States.

THE YEAR WAS 1888. Ed Burrows and his small family left Valle Verde, the Verde River drainage basin near the cliff dwellings known as Montezuma's Castle, and traveled by foot toward Prescott, where they had determined to settle. A long journey on foot was not an unusual undertaking for pioneers, but the Burrows family met with a disaster. An unseasonable snow began to fall, first gently, then harder and harder, until the winds of a blizzard began to drive the snow.

Deep drifts hid the road and storm clouds darkened the sky into night long before the distant sun had set. The little party staggered on in deep snow and wandered far off the blanketed road into the wilderness. They were about to drop from cold and exhaustion when Mrs. Burrows saw a light ahead, through the slanting snowfall. Thinking they had found a cabin, they stumbled toward the light, but were terrified by what they saw.

A small girl, dressed in a white gown, stood silently in the snow holding a lantern. She couldn't have been more than four years old. Who would have sent a small girl out in such a storm? The Burrows family gathered around the calm little girl. She looked up at Mrs. Burrows and spoke.

"My name is Angelina..."

The girl moved through the snow, away from the family, almost as if she weren't touching the earth. The Burrowses followed. The girl spoke again, but the family could not agree on what they had heard her say.

Did she say, "Help me," or "I'm lost, too"?

They followed the pale lantern light through the blinding snow. They tried to catch Angelina, but she always stayed ahead of them, swinging the lantern as she led the Burrowses on for hours. Angelina was running as if she were lost in the snowstorm herself, but the Burrows family followed faithfully.

Suddenly a bright flash of lightning—rare during a snowstorm—blinded the family. When they opened their eyes, the little girl with the lantern was gone. The blackness of night swallowed them up as thunder rolled off the distant mountains. The wind laid low and the snow began to drift gently down again, as it had hours before. Without the wind, the stillness seemed warm and the family sought shelter under an overhang, where they slept the night.

At first light, Ed Burrows saw that they had been led back to the road and were very close to Prescott. He woke his family and led them through the snow onto the road. They walked on into Prescott without seeing what Ed had seen at dawn.

Just where they had slept there was a little grave surrounded by a small iron fence. On the pink marble headstone were the words:

Angelina

Born 1881—Died 1884

La Llorona

*This story about the crying woman comes from Texas,
New Mexico, Arizona, California, and northern Mexico.*

ONCE THERE WAS a poor woman whose husband had
died in an accident, although some say he was murdered.
The woman mourned for a long time, and worked hard to
raise her two children. As time went by, however, she began
to be interested in the love of a man again, and she found
that a young Spanish rancher was paying more and more
attention to her in the marketplace. One day, the young
gentleman came to her in the market and invited her to his
fine ranch house, but asked that she use the servants'
entrance. This the woman did and after many such secret
visits, during which the young rancher treated her very
kindly, she found she was in love with the man.

One night, as the two sat opposite each other, holding
hands across a fine polished banquet table where they had
eaten a romantic and delicious meal by candlelight, the
young rancher told her that he loved her.

87

She told him how much she loved him also and suggested that they should be married. The young rancher drew back his hand.

After that, he invited her less frequently and treated her less well. At last, he told her that he could never marry her because he was a rich landowner and she was a poor person of no important family. In fact, her family was an important one in the village from which she came, but that meant nothing to the rancher.

As she begged her lover to reconsider, he cast about desperately for something to say that would end their relationship forever. At last he thought he knew what to say. He told her that he could never marry her because she had children by her previous marriage, and these children would challenge the inheritance of any children the two of them might have together.

The rancher left the room and the woman, weeping, left and returned to her poor little house. There her children were happy to see her, but she saw only two stones that stood in the road to her happiness.

She led the young boys to the irrigation ditch not far from their house and told them to bathe before going to bed. When the boys were in the shallow part of the ditch, she came to them and very tenderly carried them out into the deep water along the opposite bank. There she lowered them into the water and let them drown.

Now, she imagined, she could marry the rancher.

She ran, dripping with water, to the home of the young wealthy man. She demanded admittance at the servants' door and ran past the butler to the man's bedroom. There he was kneeling at prayers. She tracked mud from her sandals as she ran to him and told him in a crazed voice what she had done.

Instead of being pleased, the rancher was horrified! He struck the woman and called for his servants to drag her out the front door. He rode his horse to the church and awoke the priest to confess his sins and pray for his soul, and the souls of the murdered boys.

The woman, driven from the ranch house by the servants, wandered the streets, crying and screaming. She staggered to the deep irrigation ditch and saw the bodies of her sons floating there.

She lost what was left of her mind.

Now, at night, along the waterways, drainage ditches, and irrigations ditches, you can see an old woman wandering in a ragged white dress. She is crying softly and calling almost in a high whisper, looking for her sons.

And if you have been a sinner, she will come toward you. At first she will look to you like a beautiful, kind lady with a sweet smile, but as she reaches where you are standing, she changes to her true form.

Her face becomes a rotting skull with stinking flesh hanging off it and hollow, burning eye sockets. She can take your soul along with her to wherever it is she goes, and she will cry.

She will cry for herself ... for her dead children ... and for your lost soul. She is the crying woman.

La Llorona.

The Curse of Kilauea

*From Hawaii comes this most believed of legends. And
the post offices there really do receive hundreds of packages
a year, just as described here!*

ON THE BIG Island, the easternmost of the Hawaiian
island chain, in the shadow of Mount Mauna Loa, is the
mighty volcano Kilauea. Kilauea is the home of the goddess
Pele, the spirit of the volcano, the spirit of fire. The legends
say that Pele and her sister, the goddess of the sea, quarreled, and Pele left home to find a new place to live. On
each of seven islands, Pele dug a pit house to live in, but
each place she dug, she hit sea water. Since fire and water
will not mix, Pele moved on to the east.

At last, Pele found the Big Island, called Hawaii, from
which the island chain takes its name. Here Pele dug deep
and did not hit sea water. Here she dug her pit house and
here she lives, at the bottom of the volcano.

Big Islanders always warn tourists not to take souvenirs
of lava rock or sand from the area around Kilauea. You may

take home seashells, which are from the sea and are the property of Pele's sister, the goddess of the sea, but you must not take lava or sand, for these are the property of Pele, the spirit of fire.

Every year, tourists come to Hawaii in their flowered shirts and golf hats. Every year the Big Islanders warn them not to take lava rock or sand as a souvenir. Every year someone ignores the warning and says it's all just a scary legend. Every year someone takes lava rocks home and it begins—the curse of Kilauea.

Their luck turns bad. They have a car wreck or their house burns down and nothing is left after the fire but the lava rock they brought from Hawaii. Or their bike breaks down. Or their dog runs away. Or their math grades get really bad.

And there are nightmares.

Nightmares about fires. Nightmares about things that move around in the darkness of the room. Things with burning, red eyes.

There's only one thing left to do.

Take the lava rock, or the sand, and pack it in a box.

Then mail it back to Hawaii.

You may laugh at the curse. You may say that you would never believe in it, but others do—the ones who know, the ones who took the lava rocks. And mailed them back.

Every year the post offices on the Big Island receive hundreds of packages of lava rock or sand being returned by new believers.

Believers in the curse.

The Curse of Kilauea.

The Lady in White on Mount Hood

This short legend is popular in Washington and Oregon.

ALONG THE COLUMBIA River the mountains look a lot the same; the roads that wind along the steep sides of the Northern Rockies also look pretty much the same. But one hitchhiker along the roads knew the difference.

She was a lady, a pretty lady, dressed in an old-fashioned dress, very neat and clean and white. She stopped cars along the western slopes of Mount Hood in Oregon and asked for a ride. She always sat in the back seat, saying that was fine for her.

No matter what the driver wanted to chat about as they rode along, the subject always turned to the mountains in the distance to the north.

"There will be danger...." she would say. "There will be

trouble...." she would say. No one ever knew what she meant.

They never knew where she went, either.

At a certain point along the road the lady in white would just disappear from the back seat. When the driver looked around, she would be gone!

Weeks after her hitchhiking began, across the Columbia River in Washington, Mount Saint Helens exploded in the most violent volcanic eruption in centuries. Most people say this was what she was warning drivers about, this lady in white on Mount Hood.

The Ghost People

The Netsilik Eskimos tell this story in Alaska and northern Canada.

WHEN YOU WALK across the wide sheets of ice and into the hard snow, sometimes you see someone else's tracks, even when you know there is no one else around. You kneel down and look at these footprints, but you do not recognize them. These are the tracks of the Ghost People, invisible people who move about us all the time, like our shadows on a clear, starlit night.

The Ghost People have bodies just like ours and use the same kind of curved-bladed *ulut* knife that we do, but they cannot be seen. Sometimes you can even pass an igloo they have built, but you will never see the invisible people themselves until they die. Then, they become visible to us.

Once a ghost person saw a beautiful woman of the *Netsilikmiut*, the Netsilik Eskimo people. He could not resist the temptation and touched her to get her attention. They fell in love even though she could only hear the sound of his voice. They were married and lived happily for many years. The invisible man was a good husband to the Netsilik woman. He hunted and brought them food and used his *ulut* to cut snow blocks and build them a good igloo to live in.

As time went by, the woman could not bear not knowing what her husband looked like. Finally, she took the *ulut* while he was sleeping and cut where she knew he was lying. Slowly the dead man became visible. He was young, strong, and handsome, everything a woman might want her man to look like. But he was also dead and the woman realized how foolish she had been. She knelt beside the body and began to weep.

The invisible people knew that one of their people had been killed and came out of their faraway igloos to the igloo of the weeping widow. Their bows and arrows moved in the air as they traveled like tufts of light fur floating on the wind. The bowstrings stretched back as the invisible people notched their arrows to shoot the woman. Some of her family were nearby, and they came to the sound of her weeping.

The Netsilik men stood with their harpoons raised, looking into the empty air where the invisible people drew their bows. The arrows were aimed at the woman and her brothers and cousins, but the Netsilik did not throw their harpoons. Slowly, the invisible people lowered their bows and relaxed their bowstrings.

The leader of the invisible people spoke with the oldest of the Netsilik men. They made an agreement: the Ghost People would never again have direct contact with the Netsilik people. Should their paths cross, they would not touch or speak.

The arrows disappeared back into the invisible people's

clothing, and the bows floated away as they walked back across the snowpack. There was no battle and everyone returned to their everyday lives. The invisible people went back to their igloos, and the Netsilik went to bury the dead man.

Now, as you walk alone, or just before you fall asleep, you may hear a sound like distant voices. If you call out to see who is there, these night voices will not answer. They are the Ghost People, and they will no longer speak to us.

Children of the Glacier

The Eskimo people of Alaska and Canada tell this story about ghostly children in the ice.

LONG AGO IN the great northwest, in the land we now call Alaska, there would come times when a sheet of ice would move slowly southward, covering the land. When the glacier came, the Eskimo people would pray to the Spirit of the Glacier. A hunter would paddle out into the freezing sea in his one-man kayak, or a group of men would go out in an oomiak (a large open boat) to catch fish for the villagers to eat. The very best of the catch would be taken to the mouth of the glacier and offered to the spirit.

"Spirit of the Glacier," the villagers would pray, "come not close to us!"

The Spirit of the Glacier took pity on the villagers. Although it would not stop its endless crushing advance toward the sea, the spirit warned the people in a voice like the booming and cracking of ice. "Take your families and get out of my path," boomed the spirit, "for I am coming to cover your village. Go now, for this night I will move quickly!"

The people went back and emptied their igloos. They put all their belongings on their sleds and hitched up their sled dogs. Everyone was ready to leave the village.

One old grandmother lived in an igloo very near the mouth of the glacier. She had many grandchildren in her care.

"I will not go," she said. "This is my house. These are my grandchildren. I have always lived here. I will not go."

The hunters told her the words of the spirit, but she would not listen to them. She turned her back on them. All the people were gone by sundown—all but the old woman and her grandchildren. As they camped far down in the snow-filled valley, the people were awakened that night by the creaking and moaning of ice on the move. Loud cracks and deep booms echoed off the blue-white snow and into the black sky.

The next morning the great wall of ice had come down the valley and stood behind them, cold and silent, all the way to the sea. They cut blocks from the fresh snow and built new igloos. They made a new village at the side of the glacier. They went out in their oomiaks to fish along the face of the glacier where great sheets of ice dropped from time to time into the sea. The Spirit of the Glacier had stopped stirring and now lay silent. The men fished in the sea along the face of the ice.

But not for long did they fish near the ice face.

One man in a kayak came near the wall of ice and a small arm made all of ice reached out and tried to grab his boat. A whole family in an oomiak saw a young boy, made all of ice, jump from the top of the glacier, fall back into the ice, and disappear, as if people in the glacier were playing the blanket-toss game. People who came near the ice saw ice people moving inside the glacier, but only when they did not look straight at the ice. When they looked straight at the ice, the ice people could not be seen.

The villagers stayed away from the glacier after that. They were afraid of the old woman's grandchildren swallowed by the ice.

They were now the Children of the Glacier.

The Thing
in *Lac De Smet*

In northern Wyoming and southern Montana they tell many different versions of this tale.

NO ONE REMEMBERS what the small, still lake was called before Father De Smet came to preach to the Indian people of the Big Horn Mountains of Wyoming. French-speaking Indians named the shallow, waterweed-clogged sink *le Lac De Smet* in his honor. Lake De Smet lies between the Piney Creek and the Clear Creek, which empty into the legendary Powder River near Fort Phil Kearney, where Indian and European people fought for control of the Big Horn region. People from both sides of the conflict told stories about duck hunters or swimmers being pulled under the lake and never surfacing. Most people blamed it on the tangle of waterweeds below the surface.

But there is another story as well.

Because lakes are few and far between in the region, wild ducks settle on the lake by the thousands to spend the night as they wing their way from Canada across the Rockies in yearly migration. When the ducks rise off the surface and take flight, they create strange shapes of flapping wings and rising bodies.

Hunters and fishermen have seen the ducks suddenly rise up as one, ten thousand wings beating, off the lake. Some say they have seen what startled the ducks into flight—a huge serpent with a long reptilian body and a head with long jaws and thousands of shining teeth. Though quickly hidden by the movement of the ducks, the serpent is said to clamp its jaws onto a dozen ducks and sink below the surface.

The Indian people told of the thing before the Europeans came. The cavalry and settlers repeated the story when they saw the thing rear its head in the heavily alkaline lake. The creature was seen several times at the turn of the twentieth century, before the lake was impounded into an irrigation reservoir in 1922.

Some local residents who had seen the sea serpent told friends or family members, who suggested that it was an illusion created by the many ducks taking wing, but others claimed to have seen the monster at times when the lake was free of the migratory birds.

Most folks who live in the area laugh at the old stories, or at least say the thing hasn't been seen since before World War I.

But others still sit beside the lake on a dark night and tell about the Thing in Lake De Smet.

The Ghost of Prairie Rose

From Wyoming comes this true story about America's first rodeo queen.

THERE IS DEEP snow in the mountains of Central Wyoming, the wind blows steadily, and the snow whips around you like sheets on a laundry line. Out of the freezing wind and blinding, stinging snow you hear a distant voice calling.

"Help me ... help me..."

Go and check on the voice if you are brave enough; it might be someone in danger. But it may also be someone who is beyond help, someone who died in 1932, someone who is now known as the Ghost of Prairie Rose.

In the 1920s, the best-known and best-loved lady bronco rider in rodeos and wild west shows was the strong and beautiful Prairie Rose Henderson. She began riding in

C.B. Irwin's Wild West Show under her maiden name of Ann Robbins. Later, she rode in the Tex Austin Rodeo for her biggest fan, Queen Mary of England, in 1924.

Her strawberry-blonde hair and prairie birthright gave her the name Prairie Rose, and Henderson was the name of her first husband. She later married Johnny Judd, a trick rope artist, and appeared in silent films with him.

She was married a third time, to Charles Coleman, a Rawlings rancher, and faded from public life.

Then, one unnaturally cold winter, in December of 1932, while Charles was away from the ranch house Prairie Rose went out to check on some of the animals. She penned the dogs in a shed to keep them warm, took a knotted rope, and went out to rope a lost horse.

Over the Green Mountains rolled a huge blizzard, and Prairie Rose disappeared.

The folks in the area searched and searched for years, but didn't find a trace. Then, seven years later, men fighting a grass fire on the prairie found a skeleton under a small bush, where someone had sought shelter quite some time before. The clothing and bits of hair were identified. They were the mortal remains of Prairie Rose.

But people in Rawlings that hunt or hike in the mountains say her immortal spirit can still be heard as her ghost walks the grassland and mountains forever.

The Skull in the Road

This is a popular story in Southern Colorado and Western Kansas, and anywhere else where Mexican-Americans live.

LONG AGO IN the mountains of Colorado there were many people who disappeared and whose bodies were never found; they fell down mine shafts, were killed by Indians upon whose land they trespassed, were murdered for their gold nuggets. So it wasn't much of a surprise to be walking along a dirt path in the hills and come across part of a skeleton, uncovered by the spring rains.

No one was surprised if they came upon a skull lying in the road; but they *were* surprised if, after they stepped over it, walked on, and looked back, it was sitting in the road right behind them! There was a skull that did this.

If you saw it and walked past, went twenty steps or so and turned around, it was right behind you. You could never see it move, but when you looked back it was right behind you, looking at you.

The only way to get away was to run off the road and through the rocks. The skull couldn't follow you there.

One day a man named Juan was walking along the path. He came around a corner and there was a skull lying in the road in front of him, its hollow eyes toward him. Juan stood for a moment, and remembering the skull that follows you, decided to give this skull no chance to do that.

Juan stepped forward and gave the skull a hard kick. The skull sailed far ahead of him and landed in the road again.

Juan walked up and spoke to it. "Well, Señor Skull, I don't seem to be able to get rid of you."

Out of the skull came a voice, deep like the roaring of a fire. "How rude of you, Señor Juan, to kick me for no reason."

Juan dropped his pack and stepped back in fear. But, realizing he ought not to show such fear in the face of something supernatural, he quickly spoke again. "You startled me, Señor Skull. I did not realize what a wise and able skull you were. I apologize for kicking you. It was thoughtless of me. Allow me to make it up to you. Please come to my cabin this evening for supper."

Thinking that the skull could not travel so far in so short a time and that without a lower jaw the skull could not eat much at all, Juan tipped his hat and went quickly on his way.

He had almost forgotten his unnatural conversation as he sat at his table in front of the fire in his cabin, his stew boiling in a pot. Then, there was a knock at the door.

Juan's hands trembled with fear as he walked to the door and opened it. Outside, there lay the skull on the ground, its hollow eye sockets staring toward him. Then from alongside the door frame, out of the darkness, stepped a skeleton without a skull, wearing a long winter cloak. The skeleton bent down and picked up the skull and set it on its neck of bones. The skeleton pulled a lower jawbone out of a pocket in the cloak and fastened it to the bottom of its skull.

Eyeballs slowly rose into the eye sockets and looked at Juan. The lower jawbone worked as the skeleton spoke.

"I have come for supper, Señor Juan."

Juan stepped back and the skeleton came in and sat down. Juan put two bowls on the table and, with his hands shaking, filled the bowls with stew. Juan sat, nervously, and watched the skull. It lifted one spoonful of stew to its teeth and poured the stew over the jawbone. Incredibly, the stew disappeared, but Juan could never figure out where it went.

At the end of the meal Juan pushed his bowl away and looked at the skeleton.

The skull spoke again. "Now that I have enjoyed so fine a supper in your home, I invite you to join me for supper in my home." The skeleton stood, bowed politely, and walked out the door.

Juan breathed a huge sigh of relief.

One week later, on Sunday, Juan was walking past a graveyard coming home from a visit to town. Suddenly, he heard something call his name. He turned and looked in the dim light of dusk, and saw the skeleton in the long cloak standing among the gravestones and crosses. The skeleton waved its arm slowly, gesturing for Juan to come in. No matter how hard Juan tried, he could not keep from turning.

He could not keep from walking through the gate of the graveyard.

He could not keep his feet from walking slowly among the stones, approaching the skeleton in the cloak.

A moment later, Juan stood before a grave with a capstone of hewn rock. The skeleton bent down and lifted the horribly heavy stone without any seeming effort. As the stone rose up, like a trapdoor to a basement, a deep red light poured out. Smoke, with the smell of burning sulphur, billowed out from of the grave.

"You made me welcome in your house, Señor Juan, and now I make you welcome in mine," said the skeleton, gesturing downward into the flames below.

Juan stood, paralyzed with terror, sweat streaming down his face from fear and the incredible heat of the fires below the earth. With much effort, Juan spoke. "Is ... there ... any ... way ... I could decline your kind invitation?"

The skeleton stood motionless for a long time. The flames licked up out of the grave. Then it spoke very slowly, "Never show disrespect for the dead."

Juan shook his head, slinging sweat in all directions. "I swear I will never disrespect the dead again."

The skeleton let go of the stone, which fell with a huge *thud,* smothering the flames. The skeleton fell into two hundred separate bones that rattled and clattered as they hit the earth. The long cloak dropped to the dirt, empty.

Slowly Juan picked up the bones and wrapped them in the cloak. He struggled to lift the stone, under which there was nothing but a small, shallow hole, cold and stinking. Slowly Juan laid the cloak full of bones into the hole and ever so gently lowered the stone over the hole. The edges of the stone cut his fingers and his blood ran down the capstone and dripped into the hole as he lowered the stone, but he dared not drop it. The stone touched the earth as silently as falling rose petals.

Slowly Juan stood up and walked out of the graveyard.

The Bloody Benders

This story is based on a true series of events, and comes from Eastern Kansas, Missouri, and Iowa.

A TRAVELER WAS walking along a country road just at sundown. He knew he was nearing a house because he heard the sound of an ax falling; someone was chopping wood on a chopping block or on a stump. He followed the sound and came to a well-lit, neat-looking house. He knocked on the door and a pretty girl opened it. She invited him in. The house was plain but clean. Supper was cooking in the kitchen behind a blanket hung over the doorway from the main room. The supper smelled good.

The traveler introduced himself and asked if he might pay for supper and a place to sleep for the night. The old man of the house shook hands with him and proposed a price, to which the traveler agreed. The wife came out of the kitchen and began to set food on the table. The daughter went to a cupboard and took out extra silver and a plate for the traveler.

110

The old man got another chair and set it at the side of the table, with its back to the blanket. "Sit here," said the old man, "in the seat of honor."

The traveler sat and was joined by the man, the woman, the daughter, and the son, who came in carrying an armload of wood for the fireplace.

Everyone bowed their head and grace was said; then the bowls were passed and everyone began to eat. There was laughter, pleasant conversation, and plenty of good food. At the end of the meal the traveler complimented the lady of the house and asked what the delicious meat was.

The son excused himself from the table and walked into the kitchen behind the blanket, carrying his dirty dishes. The woman of the house laughed merrily and smiled. "It's my specialty," said the woman, who had introduced herself as Mrs. Bender.

Behind the traveler, the son pulled the blanket aside and stepped forward with a meat cleaver. He drove the sharp blade into the skull of the traveler, who fell forward onto the table, bleeding and dead. The family lifted their dishes off the tablecloth and the father wrapped the traveler's body in it. He took all the traveler's money from his coat pockets, then lifted the body and went out the back door to the chopping block.

The son brought the ax.

A traveler was walking along that country road just after sundown. He knew he was nearing a house because he heard the sound of an ax falling on a chopping block in the distance. He followed the sound.

The Bearwalker

This is a native-American story from the chilly Upper Peninsula of Michigan and from Minnesota.

YOU MUST ALWAYS show respect for your elders and try to live within the ways of your people, or your tribe, if you are a Potawatomie or a Chippewa. If you do not, and if you insult or offend someone who knows witchcraft, then the offended man or woman will send a curse to you.

You will see him coming in the dim light of evening, under the branches of the trees of the forest. He will walk like a bear, standing on his two hind legs. His eyes will glow like the red sun at sunset. The carpet of needles on the forest floor will quiver like rippling water as the bear comes toward your lodge or your camp. You will be unable to look straight at him, this Bearwalker.

Your vision will waver as it does when you look a great distance across the water of the lake, when the sun reflects in your eyes and what you see comes and goes.

You will have to look away and he will come for you.

Nothing you can do will stop him. He will go where he will go.

He will come to you.

Depending on what offense you have committed, he may tear you limb from body as a bear would; or he may draw out your spirit and take it away so that you never find peace or happiness.

He will leave your body bloody and without its spirit, and the tracks he leaves for your family to find will be the tracks of a bear—but only of the hind feet.

You must always show respect for your elders.

JUMP!

"Jump" stories are scary tales that end with the teller yelling the last words, or screaming loudly to make the listeners jump with fear or surprise. (Obviously, this kind of story is best when read or told aloud from memory.) Here are three stories to tell at your next party or sleep-over, all guaranteed to make your listeners *jump!*

But I'm Not!

This story is sometimes called "Freshman Initiation" or other names to conceal its ending.

OUTSIDE OUR TOWN there was an old haunted house where the older boys always made the freshmen on the track team spend the night as part of their "initiation." It had been happening for years and no one thought it was anything but a harmless prank. There were five of us freshmen there that night—all alone, without any lights. We were told to split up, one to a room, and wait for dawn. We drew straws with pieces of Johnson grass from the front porch and I got the old living room, Dave got the kitchen, and so on. John was stuck going up to the dark, lonely, upstairs room.

By midnight we had heard some gravel hit one old window and some loud groans out by the shed at the back of the house, but the older boys hadn't done anything really scary, so I guess we all went to sleep.

In the early hours of morning, I was awakened by slow,

heavy pacing on the floor above me. It was John in those heavy old boots he always wore. I guess all the other guys heard it, too, because we all met at the foot of the stairs at the same time, and looked up.

There was John, or at least it was wearing John's clothes, but it had no head. It was holding a burlap bag in its hand. The thing swung the bag forward, then threw it down the stairs. We all scattered and ran. The bag hit the floor and rolled. Dirt came out of the bag. It wasn't a head. John must have been in on the joke with the older boys.

The five of us whooped with glee and ran up the stairs. It was payback time! Upstairs, we couldn't find John, but the window was open. We ran down and around the house. We found John.

He must have climbed out the window and slid down the sloping roof. The shed that attached to the house had a tin roof with sharp metal edges. I guess John couldn't stop sliding in time. There was blood on the edge of the shed roof.

John's head was lying on the roof, with its eyes open.

Dave let out a scream and ran across the back yard. He stepped on the boards that covered the old well and fell through with another scream. When he finally was found, later the next day, his neck was broken.

Bill and I ran for the well, but Bob ran into the house. When we couldn't see anything down the well, we also ran for the house to look for some light. When we came through the back door of the kitchen, Bob stepped out of the shadows with a huge, rusty knife he had found. I guess he thought we were the older boys coming in to laugh.

Bob raised the knife.

We yelled that it was us and he lowered the knife and

ran to join us. He tripped on a loose floorboard and fell on the knife.

Bill and I started running for the front porch. As I ran out into the street Bill went through a rotten board and fell through into the cellar.

I ran and ran and ran—all the way back to town.

Bob got better, but he committed suicide a few years later.

Bill was never normal again and is in a mental institution now.

A lot of people thought I might be crazy, too.

BUT I'M NOT!

Tillie Williams

This story has many versions and many names. In addition, the title "Tillie Williams" has been applied to some other stories and to a sleep-over party game.

THERE WAS A girl named Tillie Williams who lived in a great big house. She had so many friends and relatives that gave her gifts on her birthday that the gifts began to pile up and filled her room and about half the downstairs. Tillie's mother got angry and moved Tillie up into the attic, which was ten times as big as her old bedroom. All the gifts piled up there, and her dad quit threatening to throw all her stuff away.

Her bed was up there, and her dresser, and her desk to do her homework on. The only thing Tillie didn't like about her new room was that she had to climb up eight creaky, squeaky stairs to get to the attic. That was scary!

One especially scary night she went upstairs alone and got into bed to read her latest gift, a scary book about magic called *You Do Voodoo*. She didn't believe any of that

stuff, but it was fun to pretend.

As she was falling asleep she thought about what irritated her the most in life—those squeaky stairs—and she foolishly wished, "I hate climbing those old stairs. I wish somebody would come and *get me out of this old attic.*"

Then she went to sleep.

Deep in the night, when the moon was covered by clouds, Tillie suddenly awoke.

Something very heavy was stepping on the first step of the stairs to the attic, making it creak. Tillie heard a deep, awful voice whisper, "Tillie ... I'm on the first step and I'm coming to get you..."

"Dad?" whispered Tillie, "is that you?"

There was no answer. Tillie lay there for a minute, then turned over to go back to sleep.

The second step creaked slowly. The whisper came back, a little louder. "Tillie ... I'm on the second step, and I'm coming to get you..."

"Dad," whispered Tillie, a little louder, "if you're trying to scare me, I'm going to be so mad at you!"

Silence. Tillie turned over again.

Another creak. The voice was louder, like the distant howling of wolves. "Tillie. I'm on the third step, and I'm coming to get you."

Tillie grabbed her Chilly Willy stuffed penguin and covered her head with the covers.

Creak! The voice was like wind in the trees. "Tillie. I'm on the fourth step, and I'm coming to get you!"

Tillie jumped out of bed and grabbed something to throw at the thing on the stairs. She found some old Milli Vanilli cassettes.

Creak! The voice was louder, like distant thunder.

"Tillie! I'm on the fifth step, and I'm coming to get you!"

Tillie ran around the room willy-nilly, looking for something to block the door.

Creak! The voice was like a lion roaring in the yard. "Tillie! I'm on the sixth step! I'm coming to get you!"

Tillie threw away the Chilly Willy toy and the Milli Vanilli tapes and piled up all the pillows to make it look like she was still in bed.

Creak! The voice was like a snarling tiger outside her door. "Tillie! I'm on the seventh step! I'm coming to *get you!*"

Tillie crawled under her bed.

Creak! The voice was so loud it sounded like it was already in the room, "Tillie! I'm on the *eighth step!* I'm coming to *get you!*"

The door began to bend in the middle, then it broke into hundreds of pieces.

"TILLIE!" said the voice, right beside the bed. "I'VE GOT YOU!"

And then she woke up.

The Dead Man's Hand

THERE ARE MANY legends about the practice of voodoo magic. Some people believe them; others do not. I do not ask you to believe what I am going to tell. You only have to be silent ... and listen.

Deep in the American South there are people who believe in the power of voodoo. Some of these people came from Africa where a spiritual path called *animism* is practiced. Others are from different places in South America or the Caribbean, or from cities in the United States. There are believers of all races, in all walks of life, in cities and in the countryside.

Perhaps the largest body of believers lives in New Orleans, and in one dark corner of that spread-out city they gather at the grave of Marie Laveau, the most famous practitioner of voodoo medicine and ritual, whose advice was much sought after. Visitors draw small white crosses on her gravestone to bring them good fortune.

Others use the dark side of voodoo to try to bring harm to their enemies. The most powerful and evil charm used in the dark arts of voodoo is the dead man's hand.

The believer will go into a graveyard by night and find a grave that is far away from the front gate and was dug many years ago. The believer looks for a grave that is sunken, which is a sign that it is old and no one living cares for it enough to fill it in as the coffin rots away and collapses.

Then the believer takes a shovel and digs up the remains of the casket. With the shovel he lifts the lid. With the shovel he cuts off the left hand of the dead man inside the coffin.

The old dead hand is dry and mummified. The believer takes the hand home and uses it like a magic wand.

And the hand looks ...

JUST LIKE THIS!

LAUGH YOURSELF
TO DEATH

Scary storytelling sessions create tension,
and tossing in a humorous story every so
often breaks the tomblike silence and
gives everyone's bones a rest.

Dottie Got Her Liver

For another version of this story, see "Johnny and the Liver" as told by Tyrone Wilkerson in our book, **African-American Folktales.**

THERE WAS A BAD GIRL named Dottie who never did exactly what she was told. She got close, but never did exactly what she was supposed to do. She always said, "Well, it'll do."

Dottie's mother gave her some money to go to the corner store, down the railroad track just beyond the graveyard, to buy some liver for supper. Her mother told her not to cut through the graveyard and not to walk along the railroad track, but rather to go down the street (which was longer than the shortcuts just mentioned).

So Dottie said goodbye and walked on down the street until she was out of sight of the house. Then she cut through the graveyard. She saw two men digging a grave to receive the cheap aluminum casket sitting on the ground beside them. She walked over and looked at the casket.

"Go away, little girl," said one of the men, so she stood around and watched.

"Don't touch that casket," said the other man, so Dottie waited until the men weren't looking and lifted the lid. Inside was an ugly old dead woman. She must have been in a car wreck or something because her insides were all on the outside and her liver was piled right on the top. Dottie leaned in to look and fell in. The lid slammed shut with Dottie inside.

"Let me out, let me out," she yelled.

The two men thought the corpse was talking. They threw down their shovels and ran away.

Dottie pushed the lid up and said, "Yuccch!" She climbed out and walked along the railroad track to the store. At the store, she bought about a jillion pieces of candy with her mother's money, then asked for a sheet of butcher paper for her social studies project.

Dottie went back to the graveyard and lifted the lid to the casket. She took out the liver and wrapped it in the butcher paper. She walked home eating candy. She looked at the liver in the white paper.

"Well," she said, "it'll do. I don't like liver anyway."

That night, too full of candy to eat much anyway, Dottie went to bed early to read a romance novel under her bedsheets with a flashlight, just as her mother had told her not to.

Long after everyone else was asleep, Dottie heard something calling her name.

"... Dottie ... Dottie ... I'm in your house."

It was probably just the wind. Dottie went on reading. The ghostly voice got closer.

"... Dottie ... Dottie ... I'm on the stairs."

"She doesn't live here anymore!" Dottie called out. All was quiet. "It'll do," she thought.

Then the voice was even closer.

"Dottie! ... Dottie! I'm in your bedroom!"

"Dottie ate some bad liver for supper and got taken to the hospital!" Dottie called out. "I'm her adorable sister, Lottie." All was quiet again. It had worked. Dottie went on reading under the sheet.

Something tapped the sheet that was draped over Dottie like a tent.

"DOTTIE!" Something ripped the sheet off Dottie. "I'M HERE FOR MY LIVER!"

It was the ugly dead woman, with her guts hanging out and draped all around her shoulders. "WHERE'S MY LIVER?"

Dottie jumped out of bed and ran around the room. The dead woman chased her.

"Dottie," called her mother from the other bedroom, "what are you doing?"

"I'm going to get a snack," yelled Dottie, as the dead woman grabbed at her and tried to catch her.

"Why are you running?" asked her mother.

"I'm really, really hungry!" yelled Dottie.

"I'll get up and get you some nice liver," said her mother through the wall.

"I'll get it myself," squealed Dottie, running out of her bedroom and down the stairs. The dead woman chased her, flexing her rotting fingers as she tried to snatch Dottie's long hair.

Dottie ran into the kitchen, but she couldn't stop at the fridge because the dead woman was right behind her.

"Why are you running in the kitchen?" called Dottie's

mother from upstairs.

"I'm stirring the liver and onions before I put them in the microwave," yelled Dottie.

"You're supposed to stand still and stir them, silly," said her mother. "I'd better come down there and help you."

"Mom," yelled Dottie, "I don't need any ..."

The dead woman grabbed Dottie by the hair and reached for a butcher knife. "... help!" yelled Dottie, finishing her sentence.

Dottie jerked the refrigerator open and tossed the plastic bowl of leftover liver and onions to the dead woman. The dead woman took out the liver and put the onions back on the table. She walked out the door dragging her guts behind her.

When Dottie's mother came into the kitchen, Dottie was sitting at the table with the bowl of onions in front of her, holding the butcher knife and grinning innocently.

"I'm so glad you like liver," said Dottie's mother.

And Dottie had to eat liver twice a week for years after that.

Dottie frowned and looked at the plate of liver and onions night after night, and said, "Well ... it'll do."

Bony Fingers

The name "Bony Fingers" is used as the title of several different stories. This is the story most often heard using this name.

A GIRL WAS walking past a dark alley when an ugly thing jumped out at her. It was seven feet tall and had arms seven feet long. Its long, bony fingers dragged on the ground. It ran up to her, looked down at her with huge red eyes, and spoke to her with its fat, wide, blood-colored lips.

"Hi!" said the ugly thing. "Want to see what I can do with my long, bony fingers and my big, wet lips?"

"Yuch, no!" screamed the girl, and she ran.

The thing chased her all the way to the park. She had to sit on a park bench to rest. The thing ran up, dragging its fingers, and sat on the bench beside her.

"Hi!" said the thing. "Want to see what I can do with my long, bony fingers and my big, wet lips?"

"Ick, no!" yelled the girl. She jumped up and ran all the way to the stadium. She sat down on a low wall to catch her breath. The ugly thing ran up beside her and sat down, grinning.

"Hi!" it said again. "Want to see what I can do with my long, bony fingers and my big, wet lips?"

"Oh, all right," said the girl.

The thing slowly raised its long arms, closer and closer to the girl's neck. Then it drummed its fingers on its lips and said, "Bbblllbbblllbbblllbbblllbbblllbbblll!"

It Floats!

This tale is so old your great-grandparents laughed at it when they were kids.

ONE NIGHT A boy started upstairs to go to bed. He went toward the bathroom to brush his teeth, but all the lights were off and he got scared. He got to the top of the stairs and reached for the upstairs hall light switch. Suddenly he thought he saw something floating in the air in the dark hall. He heard a ghostly voice.

"It flooooats ... it flooooats...." said the voice.

The boy ran back downstairs to his mother, who was in the kitchen.

"Mom," he said, excitedly, "I went up to brush my teeth and a ghostly voice said, 'It floats, it floats'!"

"Now, don't be silly," said his mother without looking up from her eggbeating. "Go upstairs and go to bed."

So he went back up the creaky stairs and turned on the light in the hall. He walked past an open window, where gauzy curtains were fluttering in the night breeze, and came

135

closer and closer to the dark bathroom. He reached for the bathroom light switch without actually going in the room and he heard a ghostly voice again.

"It flooooats ... it flooooats...."

He ran back downstairs to his father, in the den.

"Dad," he said, out of breath, "I went up to brush my teeth and I heard a ghostly voice saying 'It floats, it floats'!"

"It's just your imagination," said his father without looking up from his newspaper. "Now go to bed."

So he went back upstairs, down the hall to the dark bathroom, and reached in and turned on the light. He stepped slowly across the room to the medicine cabinet and started to open it. Suddenly he heard a ghostly voice from inside the cabinet.

"It flooooats ... it flooooats...."

He ran downstairs to his sister who was doing her nails in the dining room.

"Sis," he gasped, "I was going upstairs to brush my teeth and I heard a ghostly voice saying 'It floats, it floats'!"

His sister said, "Don't be such a wimp," without even looking up from her fingernails. She said, "Go back and find out what floats."

So he went back upstairs, down the hall and in to the bathroom. He went to the medicine cabinet, opened it, and said, "What floats?"

And a bar of soap said, "Ivory ... Soap...."

The Viper

This ghost makes a good break in an evening of scary storytelling.

A YOUNG GIRL was at home alone on a dark and stormy night. She was reading a horror comic book when the phone rang. She answered it.

"I'm the Viper," said a distant voice over the phone, "and I'm fifty miles away." He hung up.

The girl was a little scared, but if the guy was really fifty miles away, she was sure she was safe. She went on reading. Later the phone rang again.

"I'm the Viper," said the voice, a little louder, "and I'm fifty city blocks away." He hung up.

The girl was a little more afraid, so she put down her

horror comic book and started watching a horror movie on cable TV. Pretty soon, the phone rang again.

"I'm the Viper," said the voice, even louder, "and I'm fifty yards away." He hung up.

Now she was really getting scared, so she turned off the TV and started reading a Stephen King novel to take her mind off it all. Soon the phone rang again.

"I'm the Viper, and I'm fifty feet away." He hung up.

She looked out the window at the phone booth fifty feet from her house and saw a strange man in sloppy clothes with long rags hanging from his garments. He turned and started toward the house.

The girl began piling furniture against the front door when she heard the man's voice outside.

"I'm the Viper," he called out, "and I'm fifty inches from your front door."

The girl got out her pocket calculator and figured that he was only four feet, two inches, and a pile of furniture away!

Suddenly there was a knock on the door.

"Who is it?" the girl asked fearfully.

"I'm the Viper!" said the voice outside.

"What do you want?" she asked tearfully.

"Vell," he said, "for fifty dollars, I'll vipe all your vindows!"

Bloody Fingers

The title of this story is so good that it has been used as the name of many different tales.

WHEN OLD UNCLE Finster died he left his castle in Spooksylvania to his nephew Fenestre. When Fenestre arrived in Spooksylvania, the executor of Uncle Finster's estate, a lawyer named Ventana, read Uncle Finster's will. It ended with this sentence.

"... and above all, nephew, you must never open the door to the seventy-seventh bedroom on the seventh floor, which has been locked for seventy years."

After everyone had left, and Fenestre was alone in the castle, he couldn't resist the temptation. He rode the elevator straight to the seventh floor and went down to Room 77. He unlocked the seven locks with seven of the seven hundred keys on the key ring his uncle had left him.

He opened the door.

A long, bony hand reached out at him as he opened the door. The ghoulish hand had horribly bloody fingers. A

hideous laugh came out from behind the door and the bloody fingers reached straight for Fenestre's throat.

Fenestre screamed and dropped the keys which clinked and clanked and clunked on the floor and blocked the door as Fenestre ran down the hall. At the elevator, Fenestre pushed the elevator button until his index finger was bloody. Behind him the door to Room 77 opened and a tall, hideously ugly man in ragged, dusty clothes came running out. He ran down the hall and his bloody fingers were right at Fenestre's throat when the elevator door opened. Fenestre jumped in and pushed the DOOR CLOSE button until his second finger was bloody. The door slammed shut on the bloody fingers of the creature before he could get in.

The elevator went down, but there was a thud on the elevator roof. The trap door in the roof of the elevator began to open. Fenestre pulled it shut. The creature and Fenestre tugged and pulled and opened and slammed the door on each others' fingers until Fenestre's fingers were almost all bloody.

The elevator stopped and the door opened. Fenestre ran out and into the kitchen. The creature came down through the trap door into the elevator and chased him into the kitchen. Fenestre grabbed at a huge wooden block used for storing butcher knives, but he knocked it over. As he grabbed for knife after knife, dropping about seventeen of them on the floor, Fenestre bloodied his only remaining good fingers.

The creature chased Fenestre around and around the table as Fenestre juggled the butcher knives. The creature laughed hysterically.

Fenestre ran out of the kitchen and into the front hall. He ran and ran and ran. The creature chased him and chased him and chased him.

Fenestre ran into a hall marked CUL DE SAC, foolishly hoping he could get a sack to put over the creature's head. The hall was a dead end. Fenestre skidded to a stop and turned to face the creature.

The thing in rags and rust and mold and dust ran up to him, raising his bloody, bloody fingers toward Fenestre's throat.

At the last second, the thing slapped Fenestre on the shoulder, leaving a bloody handprint.

"Tag! You're it!" said the creature, and he ran away back down the hall.

The Skeleton in the Closet

This is the last and shortest of the ghost joke favorites.

ONE DAY SOME new kids at school were helping the janitor clean up down in the basement where the huge steam heating system was located. They went further and further back into the dark recesses of the basement and found a dusty door that looked like it hadn't been opened in years.

They took hold of the doorknob, which almost fell off in their hands. They pulled, but the door was stuck because the hinges had gotten rusty.

Finally, they pulled really hard and the door swung open. Dust poured out in a cloud. When the dust cleared, the kids saw a horrible sight.

There, slumped over against the wall, was a rotten skeleton.

They called the janitor, who called the police.

For a long time no one could figure out who the skeleton had been. Then, finally, they were able to identify the rotten tennis shoes, and knew who it was.

It was the 1954 school hide-and-seek champion.

OUR FAVORITE
HORROR TALES

Horror is very unnatural fear; in these stories it is fear of the unnatural beings and events that come to haunt the lives of these victims.

Give Me Back My Guts!

This terrifying tale is told by Hispanic storytellers in the United States and some foreign countries where Spanish is spoken.

THERE WAS AN old woman whose husband had died. They had owned a very large plot of ranchland with cattle on it. After the husband's death, the next-door neighbor, who owned a large ranch of his own, began to court the widow. He fooled her into thinking he was going to ask her to marry him, and then into signing a paper deeding her ranch to him. After the paper was signed, the neighbor came calling less and less often, and finally announced he had changed his mind about marrying the widow. He gave her a small amount of money for the land and left, laughing.

The money didn't last long and soon the widow had nothing to eat in the house. She was sitting by the fireplace, looking at her big, black, empty cooking pot when she heard the cattle outside on the ranchland that had once been hers. The cattle were lowing, calling as they often did at sunset. It wasn't a *moooo* like in the comic strips; it sounded more like *ah-oooo-ah*.

The old woman had an awful idea. Poor people often ate a stew called *menudo,* made of the cheapest meat in the open-air market—cow intestines. The widow decided to take her biggest butcher knife, go into the pasture next to her house, cut open the belly of a cow, and as the cow bled to death, cut out the guts. Since wolves killed cows by tearing their bellies open, it could be made to look like wolves had killed the cow. The fine steak meat would rot, causing the neighbor to lose a lot of money, and the widow would eat the *menudo* she made in her pot without anyone suspecting her of killing the cow.

The old woman laughed to herself and got her butcher knife. She wrapped her shawl around her because it was getting dark and was going to be cold outside. As she blew out the candles and started out the front door, she saw a procession of people coming down the road.

Six men were carrying a coffin on their shoulders, headed for the graveyard just down the road. Six old women were walking behind the coffin, wailing and crying with grief. The widow knew all six of these women and knew they were not related to each other, so they couldn't be relatives of the poor dead person. The dead person must have had no family living in the area to mourn his death; or, maybe, the dead person was so hated by everyone that no one had come to the funeral. Either way, the gravedigger had offered to pay these women to follow the coffin and pretend to mourn. And the dead person, who had no family or was hated by his neighbors, had been rich enough to leave money for a fine burial.

Suddenly, the widow realized that only one person in the

village was both rich and hated. It was her next-door neighbor who had tricked her out of her land.

The widow pulled her shawl up over her head and ran out to the road. She joined in and pretended to cry and wail along with the other women, who ignored her. She followed the procession all the way to the graveyard. It was almost dark. She stepped aside and hid behind a tall gravestone as the little funeral procession came to a stop at a large, stone burial vault.

The six men, one of whom was the gravedigger, put the coffin into the stone vault. The gravedigger paid the six women and looked around for the seventh woman he had seen join the line. When he could not find her anywhere he just shrugged and went back to the vault as the women spat on the ground—to show how they really felt about the dead man in the coffin—and left. The gravedigger and his men tried to lift the heavy stone lid for the vault, but they couldn't. It weighed too much. The gravedigger paid the other men and told them to return the next morning; he would hire more help and they would get the lid on the vault then.

No one cared that the dead rancher would "sleep" without his "covers" that night.

After the men were gone, the widow came out from her hiding place and walked over to the vault. She reached in and used her knife to pry up one of the boards in the coffin lid and to cut out the dead man's guts to take home for making *menudo*.

Back at the house, she built a roaring fire. Outside, it was completely dark and clouds hid the moon and stars. She put the big pot on the fire and poured in water to make stew. Outside, the wind began to blow, as if a storm was

coming up. She put in the onion, chili peppers, and corian-
der leaf for the stew. Outside, in the distance, the neighbor's cattle, afraid of the storm, began to call.

"*Ah-oooo-ah*," said the cattle. "*Ah-oooo-ah*."

The widow tossed the guts into the pot and the water
began to boil. The cattle outside lowed and called.

"*Ah-oooorah*," they seemed to be saying. "*Ah-oooorah*."

The fire burned brighter as the wind began to blow
harder across the top of the chimney. The branches of the
trees beside the house began to scrape against the window
shutters as the wind blew the trees about. The cattle called;
it almost sounded like a word...

"*Asa-oooorah*," they seemed to say. "*Asa-oooorah*."

The gate of the fence banged open as if someone were
coming into the yard. Was it merely the wind? Heavy
sounds came from the front yard as if something huge was
walking toward the front door. Was it the trees hitting their
branches together?

"*Ah-sah-doooo-rah*," said the cattle in the distance. It
sounded to the widow like the Spanish word *asadura*, the
word for *guts*.

"*Asadura*."

Something huge and horrible began to knock on the
front door, as if to break it down.

"*Asadura!*" said a deep voice outside. "Give me back
my *asadura!*"

The old woman was terrified. It couldn't be the trees
knocking on the door. It couldn't be the cows calling for
asadura. It could only be...

It sounded like the thing was walking around the house,
shaking the window shutters, trying to get in. The old
woman lifted the pot with an iron hook and took it off the

fire. Something shook the chimney itself and sparks flew from the fire. The widow carried the heavy pot to the front door. The shutters rattled on the other side of the house, like the thing was trying to get in there. The woman sat the pot down and lifted the heavy latch that locked her front door.

The sounds were getting closer to the front of the house. The widow opened the front door and wind and rain blew in. She lifted the pot with the hook and set it outside. Something scraped along the wall just outside the door. The widow pushed the door shut against the wind and dropped the latch back in place just as...

Something heavy hit the door, making it bend inward.

Suddenly, the wind died down. The rain stopped. The cattle were silent. There was no sound at all.

Slowly, the widow reached for the door latch.

"It must have been the wind ... and the cattle..." she whispered to herself. "It couldn't have been..."

Slowly she lifted the latch.

Slowly she turned the door handle.

Slowly she opened the door.

Outside, by the light of the fire behind her, she could see the big, black pot.

And it was empty.

The Scout and the Snake Eggs

Around the campfire at Scout camp, this story is told over and over, year after year.

THERE WAS A Boy Scout who thought he knew everything. He hiked and camped and read everything he could about the outdoors. He even bragged that he could live off the land, just like the pioneers, if he had a chance.

Finally, some of his fellow Scouts got tired of listening to him and bet him twenty dollars that he couldn't even get through one full night and day without going to McDonald's for a burger. They all pitched in their change and shook hands on the bet. The Scout, with no food or water, went deep into the woods, near a stream. The other Scouts had searched both him and his knapsack to make sure he wasn't carrying a Snickers or anything.

At first the Scout pitched his tent and set up his camp.

155

He could do that well enough. Then he began to forage for wild food. None of the leaves looked like the ones he'd read about. He tried about ten different kinds of nuts and berries, and didn't much care for any of them. He set a snare and caught one whole leaf in it. He hunted for animals' holes, but nobody was home in any of them. He searched for tracks, but found mainly tennis shoe marks, mostly his own. Finally, he went to bed hungry.

The next day wasn't any better. He got a handful of fur off the end of a squirrel's tail, but couldn't catch the squirrel itself. He found a lot of rabbit signs, but no rabbit. He scared the heck out of a lot of fish, but didn't catch a one. He peeled the bark off three or four kinds of plants and didn't find any he liked.

Finally, as he was getting a drink from the stream, wondering where he was going to get twenty dollars to pay off the losing half of the bet, he saw a nest!

The eggs were strangely round, not oval-shaped like most birds'. They were a pale white, too—not brightly colored like bird eggs ought to be. And they were kind of leathery instead of having nice, hard shells like eggs from the grocery store, but he didn't care. He was hungry and it was time to eat.

He couldn't get a fire started and he couldn't crack one of the eggs. He was getting desperate and he was really hungry. So he just swallowed one of the eggs whole, to see if that worked. It didn't. It tasted awful and it sat like a rock in his stomach. He gave up.

He packed up his tent, went back to the other Scouts, and told them all about how he had eaten like a king. He told them he had gathered roots and nuts and berries, caught a squirrel, and so on. They didn't much believe him, but they paid up anyway because he didn't seem hungry. Actually, his stomach was too upset for him to eat.

Back home the next day his stomachache got worse. He started taking antacid tablets for the pain. They helped a little and he figured it would all pass. The worst he could do would be to throw up the egg. That didn't happen.

The stomachache kept returning over the next few weeks. He was too embarrassed to tell anyone. He just kept taking antacids and eating more and more because he started being really hungry!

He grew thin and pale. His friends were a little worried about him, but he just bragged that he was on a diet to trim down for his next camping trip.

He began to spend more and more time in his room lying in bed with the light out and feeling sick at his stomach. It looked like he was going to be there the whole summer. He was hungrier and hungrier, and got skinnier and weaker and paler.

Finally, one day, one of his friends came over to check on him. "He's upstairs," said his mother. "He's been there since breakfast."

The friend went up and knocked on the bedroom door. No answer.

The friend went inside and in the darkened room saw the Scout lying on the bed. The friend spoke to him. No answer.

The friend turned on the light.

The Scout was lying on the bed—cold, pale, and dead. His eyes were wide open staring at nothing and his mouth was wide open. Crawling slowly out of his mouth was a long, wet snake, darting its tongue in and out, looking for its next meal.

11:11

Some kids with a later curfew have updated this story to 1:11 A.M., but this version is the best-known one.

IT WAS THE night of the big dance at the high school. All the kids were there and having a great time. Nobody noticed that the captain of the football team and his girlfriend, the head cheerleader, had left early to go out and drink beer. Their friends would have tried to stop them if they had known.

No one alive knows what happened, but somehow their car skidded off the road and hit a tree, killing them both instantly. Back at the dance it seemed, oddly enough, that everyone had the same feeling at the same time. They all turned and looked at the digital clock on the serving table.

It said 11:11.

At that instant the power went off and the dance went dark. A group of students found the wrecked car on their way home. There was a digital clock on the dash, but it wasn't flashing 12:00 like an unplugged VCR—it was flashing 11:11.

From then on, all the kids who had known the dead boy and girl noticed the time when the clock said 11:11. Night after night, for years, they noticed when the clock said 11:11.

It was as if the dead kids were trying to communicate with their friends, to warn them to take care of themselves.

And now that you've heard the story, it will start happening to you, too. You'll start noticing the time, getting the ghostly message over and over again for the rest of your life.

Every time the digital clock reads 11:11!

The White Dress

There are many versions of this story, but they usually involve embalming fluid.

IT WAS THE night before the senior prom and one girl didn't have a dress to wear. She was poor and lived in the section of town where there were many immigrants from Haiti and other island countries in the Caribbean Sea. She had gone to the neighborhood funeral parlor that same day to pay her respects to an elderly neighbor who had died. While there, she had entered a room by mistake and had seen a young girl, about her age and size, lying in a casket. As she looked down at the casket, she noticed that the girl's dress was very pretty and brand-new. It had been probably bought just for the burial.

Then the funeral director came in and said it was time to close the casket. He sealed it with a big key, like a wrench, and said that the casket would remain closed from then until the burial the next morning. After the director left, the girl went down the hall to the room where her dead neighbor was laid out.

While she was in the viewing room paying her respects, she heard a lot of crying and wailing down the hall. Someone had collapsed with grief, and everyone, including the funeral director, ran down the hall to help the family. As the girl ran by the room with the sealed casket she had an idea.

She darted into the room, opened the sealed casket with the huge, curved wrench, and quickly slid the white dress off the body in the casket. She put the key back in the socket of the casket lid and sealed the lid again.

Stuffing the white dress into her school bag, she slipped out past the room where all the crying was coming from.

The next night, she put on the dead girl's white dress and went to the dance.

As she danced with several different boys she knew, her joints started to get stiff. As time went by, her muscles too began to stiffen, and she found herself walking and dancing awkwardly. She thought maybe there was something wrong with the dress.

She went into the girl's restroom and slipped into a stall. She took off the dress and searched it all over, but couldn't find anything wrong, so she put it back on.

As she danced some more, she became colder and stiffer, until finally she was as stiff as a board. An ambulance was called and she was rushed to the hospital, where the doctors pronounced her dead.

But she was alive! She could hear every word that was being said and see everything that was happening. She just couldn't move and couldn't speak.

Soon she was lying in the same funeral parlor where the girl in the white dress had been laid out, with her family and friends coming by and weeping. She tried to move or cry out, but she couldn't.

The funeral director came and closed the lid on her casket.

The next day the casket was taken to the graveyard. She could hear the gravediggers working.

"Did you hear what happened at the funeral home this morning?" asked one.

"No, what?" asked the other, as they threw shovelfuls of dirt onto the casket.

The first gravedigger answered, "A young mortician's assistant heard a knocking sound in one of the caskets. He opened it and a young girl in a slip climbed out. She said she had been the victim of a voodoo ritual. Someone had given her a dress dusted with zombie powder, so she seemed dead when she wasn't."

"I wonder what happened to the dress?" said the other.

And then the girl in the casket couldn't hear anything else.

APPENDIX

Afterword for Parents, Teachers, and Librarians

Children of all ages love scary stories, but as they grow older their taste in frightening topics changes. After the success of *Favorite Scary Stories of American Children* (August House Publishers, 1990), we were asked by hundreds of readers and storytellers to produce a new collection for young readers aged ten to thirteen, in middle and junior high schools. The settings and circumstances of these stories shift to young adult interests: automobiles, dating, parties, being home alone at night for the first time, and going out into the wide world by day.

Many of these stories have been told almost without change for several decades; others have evolved subtly to match advances in technology and changes in our national culture. Many are from the Scots-Irish-English and German traditions, reflecting the heritage of a majority of Americans, but many others are from Hispanic, African-American, and Asiatic traditions, honoring the multicultural nation we have become and acknowledging that our strength is in our diversity.

Whereas children in the lower primary grades have a funny bone that likes to be tickled, those in the upper primary grades and preteens have a "scary bone" that likes to be frightened. The scary stories in this collection are meant to be read silently, read aloud to groups by adults or confident young readers, and, best of all, told aloud from memory and in paraphrased personal variants to eager listeners at sleep-overs, around campfires, on long automobile or schoolbus trips, and anywhere young readers, listeners, and storytellers gather.

More and more television shows, motion pictures, and comic books are turning to frightening themes that have been written by contemporary authors for no purpose other than to terrify the viewer or reader. The stories on television and in the movies are often detrimental to young people's emotional and psychological growth because young viewers have difficulty separating fact from fiction. The terror comics are often gratuitously violent and present deranged characters as anti-heroes, making them questionable reading. We believe the scary stories in this anthology, however, are beneficial to young people's emotional and psychological growth for several reasons:

- These tales have been told millions of times because they fill a legitimate need in the lives of the listeners, with each narrative holding some fragment of ancient human wisdom concealed in a cautionary tale.
- These tales are usually told in an atmosphere wherein all those present subconsciously acknowledge them as fiction, even though they do not begin with the words "Once upon a time."
- Although they can certainly be read by a reader alone

in a dark house, these tales are more often told in a group setting where the presence of the other listeners diffuses the potential of unbridled fear.

- Even the lone reader has the power to close the book whenever he or she wishes, and to act out the terrible events in each story in his or her imagination, which can temper the terror—unlike film or video stories wherein the images are fixed and invariable.

But there is a still more compelling reason to read or hear these stories: these are our modern parables, our modern cautionary tales for our young people in their formative years. The ages ten through thirteen are difficult ones for young people *and* their parents and other care-givers. Kids are spending more time away from home, and trying hard to grow up and learn responsibility. At the same time, they are still young enough to be in need of guidance, further education, and limits on their behavior.

Where castles, dragons, knights, and princesses were once the topic of their dreams and fears, children in grades four through seven are beginning to turn their interests to daily life and real life's problems.

Now they talk about getting their license and a car someday. They talk about dating and being away from home, and spend more time with their peers than with their family for the first time in their lives. Where spaceships and sailing ships were once their preferred method of imaginary transportation, now they want something sporty-looking that gets good gas mileage. Where they once dreamed of becoming president, now they just want that first date to a party or a school dance.

Where Frankenstein, the Wolfman, the Mummy, and Count Dracula once were the stuff of their fantasy fears, they now talk about, laugh about, and worry about maniacs that escape from an asylum (Is there an insane asylum alongside the darkest road in every town in America?), and about all the Horrible Things That Happen to Kids Who Aren't Careful.

While the stories in this collection may seem bloody and gruesome to adults, they are less terrible than the evening news with its stories of wars and starvation around the world. If kids can face and master their fear of the horrible things in this anthology, they will be better prepared to face the things we all actually fear, from crime to toxic waste pollution.

Even though kids say they don't want rules, and constantly test their parents, teachers, and librarians to see if the limits we place on them are firm or feeble, the fact is most people ages ten to thirteen do want perimeters and are comfortable within them, if they believe the limits are firm and fair. This is the paradox of some of these scary stories: while kids are trying desperately to break out of the limits we place on them, they tell these stories to others their age, thereby *helping to set mutual peer limits on each other.*

In almost all these stories the central characters are young people just a little older than ten to thirteen (appealing to their desire to "hurry up and grow up") who are in realistic settings (a first babysitting job, a first date) that could cause real apprehension. Good, of one sort or another, is rewarded; evil, or more often carelessness, is punished. Bad behavior is discouraged (the couple who drink alcohol die in a wreck, the boastful Scout eats an awful snake egg out of false pride) and good behavior, especially courage, is rewarded.

Young readers this age, especially the boys, will naturally talk about dating and fast cars and blood and gore whether we want them to or not. They will tell the kind of scary stories found in this book whether we approve or not. Giving them another scary anthology won't be bad for them. In fact, these stories can do them good in the following additional ways:

- Scary stories teach young people how to deal with their fears, especially the fears associated with growing up and entering a new environment, and to master them.
- All kids need to read more and learn more about other cultures and ethnic groups; a book of culturally diverse scary stories will draw a wider audience than a book about playground events or an oversimplified juvenile mystery.
- The stories in this collection invite oral retelling. This helps young people develop communication skills and gives them the chance to enhance their self-esteem by telling these stories to peer audiences.

The social messages in these stories are simple: choose friends carefully, don't stay out too late, be brave, be strong, be truthful, be loyal, heed your elders' warnings. We couldn't do a better job with platitudes or preaching than these modern parables do with no help at all from us adults. We should admire the power of these favorite scary stories of young American readers.

Acknowledgments

We wish to thank the hundreds of young readers who have asked for, or told us about their favorite versions of, the stories in this anthology. Our legend collecting began long ago, however, in the childhoods of a previous generation.

Our thanks go to Hank Hartman, Becky Anderson Hartman, Alan Epley, Sherry Dailey Epley, Jack J. Husted, Tommy Lonon, Bobby Dahms, Stan Wooldridge, David Allen Woolly, Rodney Monday, J.W. Sumner, Judith Stewart-Abernathy, and the late Michael Olin Poe and others from the University of Arkansas at Fayetteville for all those nights in the early 1960s spent exchanging scary story legends from 1950s childhoods.

Another generation of thanks goes to Tom Phillips, Terry Edwards Phillips, Paul Douglas Ford, Stephanie Dugan Sackman, Ken Teutsch, Connie High, Scott Doss, Carl Christofferson, and all the cast members of Dogpatch, USA theme park for all those nights around a fireplace in the Ozark Mountains in the late 1970s, sharing scary tales from 1960s childhoods.

For help in our research in the late 1980s and early 1990s, we wish to thank Suzanne Jauchius of Beavercreek, Oregon; Gary Dierking of Manhattan, Kansas; Teresa Pijoan of Algodones, New Mexico; and other storytellers and collectors in the selected story notes which follow.

Our thanks to Ted and Liz Parkhurst and Kathleen Harper of August House Publishers, and to Jim Moeskau and Rex Burdett of Silver Dollar City, Missouri, the craft and entertainment theme park, for their assistance and support.

Richard and Judy Dockrey Young
Stoneridge, Missouri
February 15, 1993

Notes on Selected Stories

Most of the stories in this anthology were collected over and over again beginning in 1952, and have no single source. Some of the narratives deserve further comment, or need acknowledgment of their source. These are annotated here.

The Killer in the Backseat—The editors swear we read this in *Guideposts* magazine in the late 1950s or early 1960s, but it may have already been a legend by then.

The Headless Brakeman—This story is heard at many different railroad crossings in America, but this specific version deals with the ghost light near Crossett, Arkansas. It was first told to the editors by the late Michael Olin Poe of Sheridan, Arkansas, who, shortly after he graduated from college, died as a police officer in the line of duty in Texas. See his personal narrative "Michael and the Ghost Light" in *Ghost Stories from the American Southwest* (August House Publishers, 1991).

Tad O'Cain and the Corpse—In Ireland the wastrel's name is Teig O'Kane and he visits five churches; at the third he is choked by unseen hands, at the fourth he is driven away by ghostly grave lights, and at the fifth he is relieved of his burden. In the Irish version, the gremlins or goblins are instead wizened, gray elves. For a similar story with a female protagonist, see "Mary Calhoun" in *Ozark Tall Tales* (August House Publishers, 1989).

The Phantom Ship—Originally told to us by the late Captain Resolute Godworthy (Richard Renshaw's storytelling alter ego) of Mystic, Connecticut.

Angelina—Originally told to us by Judy Pruitt, resident storyteller at Rawhide theme park in Scottsdale, Arizona.

The Curse of Kilauea—Originally told to us by Keli'i Kalemanu and La'a de la Cruz, storytellers/dancers/musicians from Oahu, Hawaii.

Children of the Glacier—Originally collected from a native Alaskan in 1960 along the Skagit River near LaConner, Washington, by Colorado storyteller and author Mary Calhoun.

The Thing in **Lac De Smet**—Père Jean-Pierre DeSmet was a Catholic missionary in the early 1800s. The Works Progress Administration's Federal Writers' Project in Subject 1472 listed witnesses to the monster as a civil engineer named Mr. Seneff, and a Mr. Barkey, father of rodeo stars Reuben and Roy Barkey. The WPA files are housed in the Wyoming State Archives in Cheyenne.

Tillie Williams—Oklahoma storyteller Tyrone Wilkerson and Ozark folklorist JoAnne Sears Rife gave us different versions of this story, which have influenced our retelling.

11:11—Tom Phillips from Hot Springs, Arkansas, first showed us this phenomenon, which is amazingly persistent. See our story note on this story in *Ghost Stories from the American Southwest* (August House Publishers, 1991).